scars that heal

A NOVEL

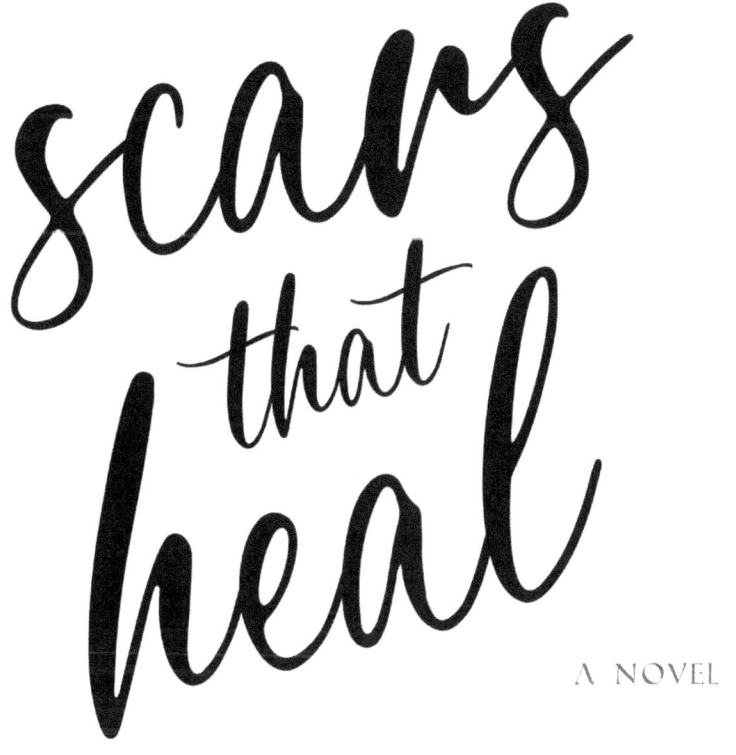

scars that heal

A NOVEL

MEGAN ASHLEY POWELL

Ambassador International
GREENVILLE, SOUTH CAROLINA & BELFAST, NORTHERN IRELAND
www.ambassador-international.com

Scars That Heal

ISBN: 978-1-64960-302-9
eISBN: 978-1-64960-324-1
Library of Congress Control Number: 2022938889

Editing by Ruthie Walker
Cover design by Hannah Linder Designs
Interior typesetting by Dentelle Design

AMBASSADOR INTERNATIONAL
Emerald House
411 University Ridge, Suite B14
Greenville, SC 29601
United States
www.ambassador-international.com

AMBASSADOR BOOKS
The Mount
2 Woodstock Link
Belfast, BT6 8DD
Northern Ireland, United Kingdom
www.ambassadormedia.co.uk

The colophon is a trademark of Ambassador, a Christian publishing company.

Acknowledgments

First and foremost I want to give all the glory to God. From a young age, my dream was to be an author, and through Him I was able to complete my first novel. I pray He uses the many messages that are within the pages of this book to change the course of someone's life.

Secondly, I would like to thank my husband Bryce for always supporting me and my dreams. Thank you for being not only a great man to do life with but also my best friend.

Next, I would like to thank my parents. Both instilled in me to chase my dreams and let God lead my life. They never told me that my ideas seemed silly and have loved me so incredibly throughout the years.

Thank you Ambassador International for taking a chance on me and publishing my book. Thank you to all my other family and friends—in someway God has used you in my life and I hope I make you all proud!

1

Lyndie

Lyndie made her way through the hustle of new students saying goodbye to their parents, meeting roommates for the first time, and hurrying to get everything done so they could move on to the exciting events the evening held. The whole first week of school at the College of Charleston was like one big party for the students. With classes not actually starting until the following week, everyone went from one event to the next. Aside from being a big university, the College of Charleston was located on the coast of South Carolina—people who didn't even go to school at the college somehow made their way there to live it up with everyone else. This was Lyndie's senior year, though, and she was over the sorority life that involved dressing up and attending parties with themes that would be seen at a middle schooler's birthday party. Now, Lyndie was as excited as the rest of them about the new, fun nightlife the college world was bringing her when she first started, but now she was ready to get her degree and be well on her way. Unlike many of her friends, she realized that there was much more to life than just these four years. And as much fun as it was living with her best friends and being surrounded by people all the time, she was ready for the future and everything it held in store.

After three years, Lyndie had mastered the whole move-in thing. She said her goodbyes to her family back home in the Upstate and made her way back to college on her own. Because she and her two suitemates were renting a townhome that came mostly furnished, she didn't really have any big stuff to move in other than her TV, some decor, and of course, her personal belongings.

She hadn't seen her suitemates all summer, and she'd be lying if she said she didn't miss them. Rachael had been her first friend at the college and actually ended up being her original roommate when they were required to stay in the dorms. Rachael was a mellow girl who had a good head on her shoulders for the most part. She had bright red hair and very fair skin. Although she had always been insecure, Lyndie constantly found herself envying Rachael for her natural beauty. She had a good personality to match it, too—she brought Lyndie out of her shell freshman year and had always been a good listener when Lyndie needed someone to cry to about anything, from schoolwork to boys. Together, they met Jodie, who lived a couple doors down from their dorm room.

Jodie did not have as good of an experience with her first roommate. Lyndie could remember one night at 3:00 a.m., Rachael got up to go to the bathroom and found Jodie huffing and turning frantically on the couch in the lounge trying to get comfortable. After Rachael had asked if she was okay, Jodie informed her that her roommate had snuck her boyfriend in their room for the night, and there was no way she was gonna sleep in the bed next to the two of them snuggled up. Rachael had woken Lyndie up and told her the story and asked if she minded if they invited Jodie to stay with them in their room on their futon. After that, the three girls became fast friends, and most nights, Jodie found herself sleeping on the girls' futon.

Jodie was the crazy one, in a good way. She loved life and was constantly making plans to do something fun and memorable. Lately, Lyndie found herself declining doing a lot of those activities, mainly because they involved parties and guys. This didn't change anything between the three of them, though—they were like sisters at this point. Jodie was very petite and had bleach-blonde hair that she had gotten cut last spring in a pixie cut. Although most people couldn't pull that off, Jodie could. She had incredible bone structure in her face and piercing green eyes, and Lyndie always told her she should have gone to school to do makeup because she did it so perfectly. There was no doubt that Lyndie stood out from her two best friends as well; her Native American heritage on her mom's side and Italian from her father's side lent her dark hair and eyes, deep tan skin, and a petite physique. Lyndie felt a thread of excitement rush through her body as she saw her two best friends standing outside their townhome. The girls rushed towards each other and embraced in hugs and laughter.

"Seriously, we can't ever go a whole summer without seeing each other again. I feel like y'all are strangers," said Jodie as she stepped back to get a good look at Lyndie. "Nope. Nothing's changed—same hair, same face, same old t-shirt," she said with a wink.

Lyndie playfully punched her on the arm.

"Somehow I doubt you could ever see us as strangers."

"All right, Jodie, let's help our little mountain girl get her stuff moved in." Rachael started walking to Lyndie's car to help get her belongings out. Lyndie smiled to herself with a lingering sadness that this was the last time she'd ever get to move in with her best friends.

2

Brantley

As summer began to fade into fall, Brantley began to feel himself relax—the busyness summer brought Outpost Marina was coming to a quick slowdown. Brantley had worked there for his senior year of high school and all three years of college. If all went as planned, the summer would be Brantley's last one at the marina. Although he was ready to move on to bigger and better adventures, it was bittersweet. His best friends worked alongside him every day; he was outside almost all day; and it didn't hurt that the money was decent for a full-time college student in the summertime. Brantley arrived at the marina for his usual twelve o'clock shift. It was just starting to get warm, and he could feel the familiar fresh breeze that blew off the water.

"There's the man; we got a big ol' party coming in today—you up for it?" Matt said before clutching his hand for the handshake they had done since they were kids.

Brantley smiled back. "I was looking for some excitement today. College kids?"

"Did you expect anything else this late in the year? Guess they are looking for a good time to welcome another school year." Chip, their other childhood friend, jogged over to them.

"Well, men, it looks like we will be the captains for the day. Get ready. I think it's gonna be a wild bunch."

Brantley rolled his eyes. Although he was a senior himself, these college festivities never interested him. He would much rather be surfing or walking on the beach with a clear and sober head. He was a very determined person, a result of being raised by his old-fashioned grandparents. They had him in church since before he could remember, and unlike most kids who grew up in church in the South, he enjoyed it and dug deep into the Scripture that was taught long after the exciting youth rallies and Sunday school doors were closed. His faith was important to him, and he credited that as what pushed him to finish school with his marine biology degree.

Brantley, Chip, and Matt all started toward the biggest boat in the marina, the one for which the reservation was made. The boat was called *Jon Jon*, named after the owner's son. They didn't get to take it out much, but when they did, they knew it would be a big party. Chip filled Brantley in on how a sorority was throwing their back-to-school bash that day. They wanted the whole package: jet skis, banana boat rides, and of course, the monster boat.

"The route is gonna take them to Folly. Some will be staying there for the weekend, but we have to stay all day in case any need a ride back to the marina by nightfall," Matt informed them.

"Are we gonna have time to make it back for the concert by the pier tonight?" Chip asked.

"As long as everything goes smoothly," Matt answered. Even Brantley had been looking forward to this concert. It was his favorite local band; they all had grown up playing Little League with the bass player, and none of them wanted to miss seeing him play. However, after learning about all the college kids who would be staying at Folly, Brantley realized it wasn't just going to be the chill concert he was hoping. Growing up in Folly definitely had its perks, but the tourism was somewhat of a downfall.

"Well, guys, let's get this party started." Matt said this with a smirk and a wink, and Brantley knew this was going to be one long day.

3

Lyndie

Lyndie had been back in Charleston barely two days, and Jodie was already trying to drag her and Rachael to one of her sorority's parties. The party didn't sound too bad; they had rented out a huge boat to take across the canal to Folly Beach for a music festival. Lyndie would have much rather driven to Folly for the day to enjoy the last bit of summer lounging on the beach. But with both her roommates on her case about going, Lyndie knew she had to go, or she would never hear the end of it. Besides, maybe if she got this party over with, she could lay low the rest of the year.

"All right, I'll go. On one condition, though: we stay at the Tides, just us three in a room, and I'm spending the weekend on the beach relaxing," Lyndie told her two friends.

"Perfectly fine with me! This is gonna be so much fun. I already reserved three tickets for us. I knew you'd end up coming," Jodie said with a snicker.

"So when do we leave?" Rachael asked, still out of breath from their routine run through downtown.

"We need to be at Outpost Marina by ten o'clock sharp—the boat leaves at 10:20." Jodie had excitement written all over her face.

"Well, I guess we need to start getting ready then. I haven't even packed," Lyndie said with a lot less enthusiasm than Jodie.

"Let's get going then. The clock is ticking, and we aren't going to miss this now." Jodie jolted past them to her room. Lyndie and Rachael exchanged knowing grins; they could only laugh at their friend's joy in everything college brought.

4

Brantley

Clusters of college students began to gather at the marina a little before ten o'clock. Brantley and the other guys he worked with were trying hard to give everyone some orderly procedures and direct people onto the boat. As more people showed up, Brantley could feel himself getting overwhelmed. And here he had thought he had left these crazy days in the summer. He occasionally glanced over to see how Chip and Matt were doing, but they seemed to be enjoying themselves. They had always liked the excitement. At some point, Brantley did, too, but now it just made him uncomfortable.

The guys and girls were piling in the boat in a steady flow, many carrying coolers, suntan lotion, and footballs, all while cranking their loud music. The boat had not even left the dock yet, and dozens of beers were being poured or popped open by the minute. Brantley never drank much—he didn't want anything as superficial as alcohol to interfere with him possibly leading someone to the Lord. He wasn't perfect, however. Throughout high school and his first two years of college, he drank casually, but he really didn't care much for the taste of it. Brantley knew to expect this party atmosphere; the same sorority threw this party every year he worked at the marina, and every year, it seemed to get a little crazier.

"Brantley, it's almost 10:20. You about ready to get this boat going?" Chip hollered. Brantley gave him the thumbs up and motioned for the crowd on the boat to get ready to leave the dock.

"Wait, wait! We're coming; we have tickets!" Three very beautiful women were walking fast towards the boat. Out of breath, the blonde one put her hand on Brantley's shoulder.

"Oh my gosh, we almost missed it—y'all really need to have clearer directions on the website. Anyway, we good to get on?" She handed Brantley her ticket and jolted past, rushing toward a group of girls and guys who all seemed happy to see her. The red-headed girl walked past and gave him her ticket. Then came her friend following behind, who he noticed was very beautiful. His face got a little warmer than usual when she handed him her ticket, slightly brushing her hand against his in the process. He watched as she retreated to the same group as her friends and couldn't help but think how she seemed out of place here. If nothing more than the fact that every girl on the boat had makeup caked on their face while she just had a natural bronze glow about her. He shook away his thoughts and led himself back up the stairs to the boat deck, found Matt, and asked who was going to be the captain for the day.

"Ah, I think Chip called dibs; he's thinking he's gonna impress some of these girls," Matt said with a laugh. Brantley didn't complain. He just wanted to sit back, relax, and pray nothing went wrong.

5

Lyndie

The boat was packed. Lyndie knew it the minute they got out of the car and could hear the music blaring, and they hadn't even reached the marina yet. However, she was used to this. She knew how to play it cool, how to put on a smile and seem like she was enjoying herself. To make matters worse, they were late, but they weren't late enough that the boat had already left. At this point, she and Rachael were basically jogging to keep up with Jodie. The marina was worn down by many tropical storms that had blown by throughout the years, but it had a charm to it that oozed that laid-back beach vibe that drew everyone there.

As they were walking towards the boat, she dug through her beach bag for the ticket Jodie had given her that morning. She wouldn't have known that the guy collecting the tickets worked there if she hadn't just seen Jodie and Rachael give him their tickets. He was around her age, and when she gave him her ticket, he gave her an impossibly cute grin. She wasn't one to be infatuated by men, even really good-looking ones, but this guy made her catch her breath. He had sandy blond hair held back in a small, messy ponytail; clear, gray eyes; deep bronze skin; and a tall, athletic build. He looked like he had just walked off the front cover of a surf magazine. She tried to smile back casually but walked away fast, knowing he had to have sensed her nervousness as she handed him her ticket. She followed her friends to a group of girls from Jodie's sorority. Another guy around their age in an *Outpost Marina* shirt came out on the top deck and told them over the intercom that they were about to take off into the waters and went over a couple rules. Lyndie started chatting with girls she knew; Cynthia, a girl in her English class, offered her something to drink. Lyndie just shook her head.

"I'm good right now." Her eyes drifted around the boat, watching all the familiar and unfamiliar faces alike. She decided to have a seat on the upper deck near the nose of the boat where it might be more relaxing.

She closed her eyes and laid her head back in her chair but was startled by a man's voice saying, "Excuse me, ma'am."

6

Brantley

He was embarrassed that he had to tell the pretty girl he'd seen walk onto the ship last minute that she wasn't allowed on the upper deck, but a part of him felt butterflies knowing it meant he'd get to talk to her. He thought it somewhat odd she was on top of this boat, anyway, when the rest of the party was downstairs living it up.

"Excuse me, ma'am. I'm sorry, but you can't stay up here. This is for the captain and crew members only. Liability," Brantley tried to explain kindly.

She looked taken aback and slightly embarrassed herself. "Oh, I'm sorry. I didn't know." She quickly jumped up and grabbed her belongings. Brantley felt a sudden urge to volunteer a little extra conversation before she walked away, something he rarely felt.

"It's okay. If you don't mind me asking, why are you up here? It looks like the party is down there."

She seemed unsure how to answer his question.

"Um, it's just not really my scene anymore; my friends talked me into coming. I just saw this up here where no one was and thought it may be a good place to get away from all that," she said, motioning below. They both turned slightly to see girls and boys, probably half of them underage, guzzling alcohol, dancing, and flirting.

Brantley nodded his head. "Sounds like something I would have done myself; big crowds aren't really my thing." An awkward silence arose between them, and he watched as she reached for her bag and began to walk away. "Just between me and you, there is a hidden place behind the cabana at the back end of the boat on the very bottom deck. I'm not sure it will drown out the noise, but at least you can be left to yourself."

She smiled back at him. "Thanks. I may just have to check it out."

He watched as she retreated down the winding stairs in search of the spot. The rest of the trip, he tried to keep his eyes on the horizon and the rowdy crowd that were partying below, but his eyes couldn't help venturing to the girl he had talked to earlier. For most of the ride, she sat on the back side of the boat facing the ocean. She read most of the time and occasionally walked back to her friends to make conversation, but only for a few minutes. At one point, Chip interrupted his thoughts.

"If I didn't know any better, I'd say you were checking her out."

Brantley rolled his eyes. "Hey, you know me, just making sure no lovers try to sneak back there for some fun."

"Mhmm," said Chip.

Maybe this trip wasn't as bad as he thought it was going to be after all.

7

Lyndie

Lyndie had to admit she was somewhat glad she had come on the trip. It was quite peaceful in a weird way; she got to catch up on some reading, and the view was beautiful. The whole way to Folly, though, she couldn't help but think about the guy who had talked to her and given her the idea of coming to the back of the boat. He was a handsome guy, but she had met many handsome guys in her day. It was his politeness that struck her. What he had said made her think he wasn't really into loud and rowdy crowds like this—a unique characteristic she didn't find much nowadays. When she saw the beach in the distance, she gathered her stuff together and went to find Jodie and Rachael. When she finally found them, Rachael still had some sense about her and asked her where she had been this whole time. Jodie, however, was completely and totally gone. She tried to get her friend to sit down with her, but at this point, she didn't even know how Jodie could function enough to get off the boat and onto the beach. She had already puked all over the shoes of the guy she had had her eyes on for a while. "All right, Jodie, I need you to come sit up for me." She began to see the water well up in her friend's bright blue eyes.

"Lyndie, I threw up on him; he's never gonna talk to me again."

Lyndie just patted her back and lied, "Yes, he will; let's get you cleaned up."

They stumbled their friend to the tiny shack of a bathroom. As soon as they entered, Jodie threw up all over the bathroom. Luckily, Rachael and Lyndie were in the clear. They made her sit on the ground and splashed water on their friend, trying to clean her up as best as possible.

Lyndie felt the boat stop, and panic rushed through her when she looked down and saw Jodie was out like a light. "Hurry, we have to clean this up a little."

"Lyndie let's just leave it. I am sure they are used to it; they have parties on this boat all the time," said Rachael.

"No, Rachael, you know me—I can't do that. Besides, what are we gonna do with her?" They both tried splashing her with water, calling her name to try and get her to wake up, but she was in a deep sleep.

They heard a man's voice come back on the intercom: "All right, people, we have arrived at Folly Beach. Thank you for being a great crowd, and please remember all your belongings. Anything left behind will be confiscated and taken back to the marina. Please leave the ship in an orderly fashion and be safe. The boat will leave at twelve tomorrow morning, and on Sunday, one will be back for pick up again at one o'clock sharp, and again, tips are not expected but always appreciated. Thanks everyone." They heard the stampede of people rush off the boat in what was obviously not an organized fashion. Both Lyndie and Rachael tried picking Jodie up, but she was limp.

"Rach, I am gonna have to get one of those guys who run the ship to help us. Goodness, this is embarrassing; never again will I be talked into something like this!" Rachael agreed it was their only choice before they were stuck on the boat. Lyndie made her way to the captain's deck. She scanned the empty boat; the only thing she saw were empty beer cans, crushed Solo cups, and bottles of sunscreen lying around. Her eyes stopped once she saw the guy who had told her about the "secret spot" earlier, who was also surveying the mess the crowd had left behind.

She had no choice.

"Hey, um, I have a friend passed out in the bathroom; can you please help us? We can't get her out by ourselves." He looked stunned. She was mortified.

"Yeah, glad to help. Is she okay? Still breathing fine and everything?" Before she could reply, he continued, "Let me go get the guys; we will be right down." Lyndie watched as he jogged down the steps to the other guys, who all came quickly to her side. As if they didn't know their own boat, she showed them the way to the bathroom they were in. She watched as they checked Jodie over and lifted her up, brought her to the nearest seat, and sat her up. The guy she had spoken to earlier tried to give her water and splashed it on her face. Jodie's eyes slowly fluttered open.

"Jodie! I'm glad you're okay! We're checking into our hotel room, and you are gonna get some rest. This is ridiculous," Rachael said with annoyance in her voice. "Can you walk to the room, Jodie? I'm sure these men would like to get back to their job."

Jodie just rolled her eyes and rested her head back against the seat and mumbled a faint, "I'm fine."

"Well, we are gonna be here all evening, anyway; and we actually live here, so I guess one of us can help y'all get her to a room while the other two stay and mend the boat," one of the guys suggested. The other two nodded.

"I can go with them," volunteered the man who had talked to Lyndie. "Where are y'all staying?"

Lyndie spoke up. "The Tides Hotel—it's right there." She pointed to the only hotel on the beach. He scooped Jodie up and led the way as he walked them to their hotel across the beach. Lyndie couldn't help but be impressed by his generosity.

8
Brantley

On the way back from carrying the girl's friend to their hotel room, Brantley couldn't stop thinking about the kindness and appreciation he saw in the eyes of the girl he had met on the boat. After he let one of her friends take over and put the girl to bed, she walked him to the door and thanked him probably a dozen times. He could tell she was mortified and frustrated, and he assured her he was used to these kinds of things after working at the marina for so long. She introduced herself as Lyndie. It suited her very well. He, in turn, gave her his name and told her he hoped she and her friends had a good weekend and for them to stay safe. He then walked back toward the boat. Striding across the warm sand, he replayed all the events that had unfolded that day. He never would have imagined he would spend the afternoon daydreaming about some college girl. He reminded himself that he was a college guy, and this was a normal thing. He tried to shrug off his thinking and assure himself that nothing would come from dwelling on it. As he approached the boat, he could hear Chip and Matt blasting reggae music and chuckling about something.

"Well, one day's hard work is done, my boys," he said, giving each of them a slap on the arm before pulling up a seat with them. "Y'all did a good job at cleaning up; maybe I should let y'all do it more often."

"And let you escort all the pretty girls around while we do all the dirty work?" Matt chimed in.

"Hey, it isn't as glamorous as it sounds, and for such a small girl, she sure did get heavy quick."

"Kinda funny how it worked out that the girl you had your eyes on all day ended up asking for your help," Chip offered.

"I told you before I didn't even notice her, other than when I had to tell her she wasn't allowed on the top deck. What's with you trying to push me to talk to girls lately?" Brantley asked.

"I'm not, dude; chill out," Chip tried to defend himself.

"So, the other night when you asked me to get dinner with you, Lena, and one of her friends visiting from Florida, it was just *because*? Or the day before that when you and Lena introduced me to that girl who was minding her own business on the beach? Seriously, I am fine being single. It's good for me, right, Matt?" Matt was single as well, and both guys were completely content with that.

"I dunno, Brant; I wouldn't exactly mind having a woman around. Definitely wouldn't complain. I am only getting older, ya know," Matt offered with a shrug.

Brantley rolled his eyes. "Well, that's all good and fine. I just really feel like it's good for me to be single. If I were in a relationship, it would take my focus off school, traveling with surfing, and God. Y'all know how it is being in your twenties and trying to serve God and keep a good head on your shoulders at the same time. It's already hard enough; mixing a girl into the picture would only make it harder."

"That is why you need to find a girl like you. Someone who has the same values and is going to encourage you, not bring you down." Chip always made good points.

Brantley just tilted his head. "Well, you make a good point. It's just finding that type of girl in this fast-paced, crazy world. I'm not gonna lose any sleep on it, though. I reckon if God wants me to meet someone, it'll happen."

Chip replied quickly, "Well you better get to trusting Him on that one; He may already have." Chip had always been his wisest friend and his go-to when needing advice, especially spiritual advice. He was a true brother in Christ to Brantley, and Chip would never know how grateful Brantley was for him.

Matt seemed to snap out of his own thoughts, "Welp, boys, I say we go home, get changed, meet the crew at around six at the drop-in to grab a bite to eat, and then head to the concert. We all need to loosen up a bit, I think." Brantley and Chip agreed to the plan, made sure the boat was all locked up at the dock, and made their way to the parking lot to head to their houses. Luckily, each of their houses was hardly a mile apart from the other.

All the locals were close-knit; it was one of Brantley's favorite parts of growing up in Folly. Ever since he could remember, he was either by the ocean or in it. His parents had always been drawn to the ocean, and Brantley guessed he must have gotten that from them. He was in board shorts and learning how to paddle out at the age of three; and by five, he was already surfing on his own. His grandparents, whom he lived with now, enjoyed living at the beach but never spent much time in the actual ocean. They mainly moved down for the laid-back atmosphere Charleston provided. He wished his grandparents enjoyed doing stuff on the water like he did, but he learned to be okay with it. They supported him and his surfing even if neither had ever picked up a board before. His dad had taught him everything he needed to know about the ocean—how to swim, surf, fish. Brantley's mom was always his own personal cheerleader, and she herself even taught him a couple of tricks on the board. She was more into scuba diving, though, which was another one of his many passions. He began to feel the familiar ping of sadness swell up in the pit of his stomach, but he made himself focus on the here and now and forced a smile onto his face. When he walked in, his grandparents were lounging in the sun room. The old house had been there for over thirty years. It was worn by many storms, but he loved it and the memories it held.

"Well, you're home early, son," his grandpa said, standing up and giving his shoulder a squeeze.

"We left the boat at the dock overnight, had to take a party over here this morning. Thought I'd come home and get myself cleaned up before tonight."

His grandmother gave him a knowing look. "Going to that concert everyone's buzzing about?" she said, flipping back through her newspaper.

"Ah, Grandma, what else is there to do?"

"Well, my *Antiques Roadshow* comes on tonight; you can help with some knitting. But I know a grown boy like yourself wouldn't be interested in spending his Friday night at home with his granny," she said, smiling her usual sweet smile. Brantley gave her a hug and went off to his room to get ready. He had a strange sense of excitement for the night ahead, a feeling he didn't often get. He liked it.

9

Lyndie

The chain of events that happened that day didn't surprise Lyndie. This was pretty normal for the life of a college student at the College of Charleston. What got to her was the lingering embarrassment. The guy from the boat who had helped them get Jodie back to the room probably thought she was just a girl who only cared about parties and derby days. But what did it matter what he thought? He was a total stranger, she kept reminding herself. Even still, it was in the back of her mind all day. She found herself doing something she rarely did—taking her anger and annoyance out on Rachael and Jodie.

She had just got done giving Jodie a huge spill on how she's worried about her, especially since college was about over and the real world was about to begin. She decided to take a hot shower to blow off some steam. When she got out, she heard Jodie laughing about the situation on the boat. Lyndie couldn't help but feel a little sad that her friend didn't even care she'd thrown up all over a bathroom and then was out cold for a good four hours. Then there was Rachael, who was always defending Jodie, saying, "Lyndie, it happens, and it's not a big deal. Next time, Jodie will know her limits, but relax and let's have a good time." She knew this would not be the last time, and it just frustrated her. She had already contemplated catching a taxi back to the mainland, but she knew that would cost more than she wanted to spend, and she had already paid for her part in the room. Also, she had to admit that she was kind of looking forward to this concert everyone was talking about that would be by the pier that night. She had never heard of the band and thought it was some local group, but nevertheless, she loved live music. She got that from her father. He always brought them to any concert he could while she was growing up, popular or not. "You're here. Let's make the best of this. What's done is done."

After she showered and got dressed, she decided to talk to the girls. When she walked in, Jodie was shuffling through her overnight bag to find something to wear, and Rachael was scrolling through her phone. They both looked up when she entered. "Hey, listen, I hate what happened today. I love y'all, and I want to have a good time, but can we all just promise to behave somewhat like adults tonight? My nerves can't handle many more days like today," she said with a grin.

A somewhat offended look spread over Jodie's face, but she knew better than to fight back.

"Yes, Mother, I will behave. Love ya." She got up and hugged Lyndie around the neck.

Rachael agreed as well, and all was right between the girls again. Rachael cranked up some old music from back when they were in middle school, and the girls sang and put on their makeup and got ready together. These were the moments Lyndie would miss most of all—the ones that made her feel like a teenager again—the small moments when she could let herself go and just have fun.

"I wonder if *he* will be there tonight." Rachael nudged Lyndie with her elbow and winked.

"Who?" Lyndie asked, trying to sound clueless.

"Don't play dumb with me. That's why you got so upset at Jodie; you were embarrassed," Rachael said. Lyndie hated when she was right about stuff.

"Whatever. I am sure he cares nothing about being around the crowd that he had to be around all day today."

"Mhmm." Rachael started singing Beyoncé's "Irreplaceable." Lyndie found herself smiling; she could tell that she cared how she looked a little more than usual, and Rachael and Jodie were catching on. They both knew her well.

10

Brantley

The usual meet up spot for Brantley and his friends was especially hopping that night. The drop-in had always been a local hangout, but during the tourist season, people from all around made their way there to try the food and listen to the live bands. Tonight, it was like tourist season all over again. The place was especially buzzing with young people in their early twenties. In the center of the place was a tiki hut bar with surfboards and old beach posters lining the walls. After the sun went down, it turned into a bar—people crowded around for the nightlife in the tropical atmosphere. It wasn't really anything special, but it felt like home to Brantley. Even though he didn't participate much in the drinking, he and his friends had been regulars ever since they were old enough to ride their longboards there to grab burgers after school. He tried to stay away during tourist season, but as soon as fall rolled back around, he and the others, both young and old, would start meeting up again—not really to drink, but to play music and hang out. However, tonight it had definitely turned into the bar atmosphere. Brantley leaned in close to Chip, his other friend Sawyer, and Sawyer's girlfriend, Ariana. "Y'all sure y'all wanna chill here? It's pretty crazy tonight." They could barely hear him over the music and the crowd of people talking and dancing.

"Well, we told Matt we'd meet him here; once he gets here, we can decide," Chip suggested.

Ariana chimed in, "Maybe one of y'all should help Jake behind the bar. They must not have gotten the heads up about the crowd coming in since he's alone; he looks like he's barely hanging on."

"I'll go see if I can lend a hand with anything, but I'm not missing the concert. Eight o'clock comes, and I'm gone." Chip went over to talk to Jake, and the group watched them disappear into the back. Brantley, Ariana, and Sawyer chatted with other friends they knew who were regulars. It was about twenty till eight when Matt finally peeked his head in.

Brantley walked over. "Come on, man. What happened to meeting at six? We've been here forever now."

"Sorry, I got caught up helping my mom get the grill going. I tried. No hard feelings?" He already knew Brantley couldn't have hard feelings toward any of them. They did their usual handshake and joined the others.

"Well, it's about time ya got here," Chip said as he walked over, sweat beads lining his forehead. "Y'all ready to hit up this concert? Ol' Jake gave me about fifty dollars for helping him tonight. Betcha wish y'all would have stepped up now, huh?" Chip laughed aloud, being his usual light-hearted self. "I'm cool with not showing up to the concert drenched in sweat and smelling like beer and greasy cheeseburger. You can have your money, man," Sawyer said. Everyone walked out and down the small mainstreet that was at the heart of Folly. It was lined with small surf shops, other dives like The Drop In, and a couple of souvenir stores. Brantley could hear the waves crashing on the shoreline well over the noise of college students buzzing in the night air, trying to soak in the lingering bits of summer. They walked underneath the pier to the crowd of people packed shoulder-to-shoulder in front of a small stage set up on the sand. They joined toward the back of the crowd.

"You see the guys yet anywhere?" Matt asked.

"Nah, they probably won't come out until right at eight o'clock. Ty told me they were gonna hang inside the pier office, do some warmups up there till it was time. Tonight's a big night for them, and I bet they're nervous," Chip said. Brantley waited patiently with the others, casually listening to everyone get into a conversation with a guy they had all gone to school with who'd moved away to Los Angeles and had recently moved back. He was telling them all about the stuff he had seen and how different of a world it was there compared to Folly.

Out of the corner of Brantley's eyes something drew him out of his daze; he felt his heart almost skip a beat. The girl from earlier on the boat and her two friends had walked up and were a couple of people away from him.

"Well, that's awkward, and pretty great, all at the same time." Chip motioned towards her. Chip's girlfriend, Dev, shot him a knowing smile; Chip must have already filled her in. Great. Now he would have both of them on his case about it.

Just then, the band started to play. "Look, they are coming on stage." Luckily, this caught Dev and Chip's attention, and he could somewhat relax again. He looked back over and saw that the girls were not there. He tried not to think about it much and to instead pay attention to the band. Ty was the lead singer, and they'd all grown up with him; he was also super talented, and Brantley knew a night like this with so many people was great for their music career.

The concert went on for about two more hours. It was great, and everyone really seemed to enjoy it. By that point, people were on all sides of them, and the crowd extended far behind them. Brantley could barely move. Throughout the night, he found himself looking around for her but didn't see her again. Right toward the end of the concert, when he could tell Ty was winding it down, he saw her. She was walking along the banks looking around frantically. Then he watched as she began to walk down alone, passing behind the crowd of people. He thought to himself that something seemed wrong and made his way through the swarm of people and walked in her direction. *What am I doing? This is weird. I'm gonna freak her out,* he kept thinking to himself. But even so, his legs kept moving in her direction. She was standing alone, looking around. He awkwardly waved her way. He watched as she squinted, trying to make out who he was and why he was walking toward her. He started to speed up his walk.

"I was in the crowd and noticed you looked freaked out. I just wanted to make sure everything was okay." A relieved look spread across her face. She must have finally recognized him.

"Oh, my goodness. The whole time you were walking my direction, I was thinking of ways I could get away if you were some random drunk dude! Totally was not expecting it to be you, but yeah, I'm okay."

He could tell she was lying but couldn't decide if it was because she wanted him to go away or just because she was embarrassed.

"All right. If you're sure. I just felt like I needed to ask."

She hesitated. "Thank you, but I'm fine. I just needed some air."

"All right, well, have a good night."

Brantley forced himself to turn around, already mentally lecturing himself on how he needed to stop worrying about other people so much. Then, he heard a shaken voice call out, "Um, actually I'm in a predicament. Maybe you could help."

He turned around; she looked desperate for some help. And with that, he let out a huge sigh of relief. Maybe he wasn't so vulnerable after all.

11

Lyndie

The night had actually been going pretty well until Lyndie realized her phone had slipped from her purse at some point during the hustle and bustle of the crowd at the concert. Once she realized it was gone, she told Jodie and Rachael and went back through the crowd trying to look for it around people's feet. At that point, she realized she was in the middle of the rave of people, and she couldn't see her friends anymore. She felt a familiar wave of panic and claustrophobia run through her. She was trying her best to get through what seemed like an endless array of strangers. Finally, she saw the sand breaking through, and she knew she was reaching the end of the crowds.

Once she was out, she walked up to the dunes to catch her breath and try to think of what to do next. There was absolutely no way she would be able to find her phone in that mess. She would have to wait until the concert ended and people started to disperse. She reeked of spilt beer. She thought about going back to the hotel but figured sitting there moping around about a lost phone would be pointless. Besides, maybe if she waited around, she could catch Rachael and Jodie as everyone left. She decided to take a walk down the beach to try and calm her nerves. Even though she was trying to relax, she knew she was pacing; and when she heard a man yell after her, she thought about running. Right when she was about to take off, she realized it was the guy from the boat who helped them take Jodie back to the hotel. What in the world could he want? And how did he even find her? When he asked if she was all right, she didn't know what to say and simply said, "I'm fine."

Surprisingly, he didn't push her and replied with a casual, "Okay, just checking. You looked lost." He then turned around and began to walk off.

She could have slapped herself. How stupid could she be? She needed someone's help. At least, she could use his phone.

"Actually, I could use some help," she called after him. He casually turned back around, and she couldn't help but notice a satisfied grin spread across his face that he was clearly not trying to contain.

"You're making me feel like superman today or something," he said to her.

"I guess that makes me a needy girl. It's definitely not been the finest day for me."

"That can always change. What's going on? Is it your friend again?"

She drew a breath, "Not this time. Ya see, in the midst of that craziness," she motioned towards the crowd of people, "I somehow managed to drop my phone. So I went looking for it, but I am a little claustrophobic and a tad freaked out when I'm alone with strangers. So here I am after fighting my way through all that, alone, lost, without a phone." An even larger smile came across his face, and she felt a bit offended.

"Phew, that's a relief. I thought it was gonna be something catastrophic. Here, ya need my phone?" She couldn't help but grin; it did sound kind of silly when she heard herself say it out loud.

"Thank you," she said, smiling at him. She took his phone and dialed both Jodie and Rachael's number. Unsurprisingly, neither of them picked up. She handed his phone back.

"No answer?" he said.

"Nope. Typical. Thank you, anyway."

An awkward silence fell between them, and just as she started to walk away, he broke the silence: "Well, it's probably not safe for you to just be walking around out here by yourself. You want me to tag along until we can find your friends?"

"You think it'll be safer for me to walk around with you, a stranger?" she said, halfway jokingly. *How had this guy shown up at the right time twice in one day?*

He shrugged. "I figure we aren't exactly strangers at this point, but suit yourself. No point in me going back to the concert now."

"Well, I was planning on walking by the ocean, too, so I guess we will both be walking down there." He seemed to catch on, and they both started toward the shoreline. He walked close to her, but not too close, giving her an appropriate amount of distance. She tried to catch a glimpse of him, only to see him looking out onto the ocean.

Interrupting her thoughts, he spoke up. "So, should I ask the awkward question that everyone hates?"

She looked at him with a questionable smile. "I don't know 'cause I'm not sure I know what you're talking about."

He cracked a smile. "Tell me about yourself. You know, the question that always makes your mind go blank and realize you may be the most boring person in the world. I've personally always hated that question, but in situations like this, it's a good conversation starter."

She took a second to think about how to respond. "Well, my life isn't glamorous, but I don't think boring is the first thought that comes to my mind," she said with a noted grin. "I'm from the Upstate—Clemson, South Carolina. And yes, although my family are all die-hard Clemson fans, I never much entertained the idea of going to Clemson for school. I always knew I wanted to go to college by the ocean, and I guess that's why I was drawn to Charleston. I'm studying to be an art teacher and finishing up my senior year." She paused. "Now, let's make this a fair game; I told you about me. Now it's your turn."

He drew in a breath. "Well, surprise, I'm actually a senior at Charleston, too—sometimes us beach bums can get into college also." He let out a cool laugh. "I'm studying marine biology; it's what my dad did, and ever since I was old enough to remember, he would take me out with him every Tuesday morning while Mom ran her women's Bible study. I fell in love with the water, the animals, the whole thing. I was blessed to know at a young age what I wanted to do with the rest of my life. I feel like God gave me a sense of being drawn to the ocean, to the creatures and life in it. I see it as being its protector, or a good steward of it all, I guess. And the more I studied it, the more I fell in love with it."

Lyndie hesitated—she wasn't expecting him to say all that. "Wow, that's amazing you feel so passionate about it. That's kind of the way I am with art, too. It's more of a stress relief for me. No matter what it is, as long as I'm being creative, I feel like I'm almost in a different realm where nothing else matters and all things are possible. I want students to be able to catch onto that, to learn sometimes it's okay to not take life so seriously." Even as she said this, it caught her off-guard that she was telling this to a complete stranger.

"Seems like you found your gift—or one of them, anyway," he said. She didn't really know what to say back to that, so she changed the subject.

"So do you think you will work with your dad once you graduate?"

He stayed silent for a second. "My dad and mom passed on when I was nine. My grandparents raised me from that point on. They never tried to take the place of my parents—they still spoil me and love me the way any grandparents would. They are the best people I know, and I don't know how I could have gotten through all of that without them—and God, of course. I owe a lot of who I am today to Him."

"Brantley, I am so sorry to hear that. I'm sure they loved you; you sound really at peace with it all."

"It's taken a while. Three years—really, even five years—after the accident, I wouldn't have been able to mention it hardly. Now, it's almost therapy. Talking about them keeps them alive in my heart. And now that I have grown deeper in my relationship with God, I know now, more than ever, that they are safe with him. I'll see them again, and that's what gives me peace—knowing I will talk, laugh, hug them again; it's hard to be very sad when you know that."

Lyndie felt herself get uncomfortable. Although she had grown up in church, her faith wasn't something she thought about too much. She believed there was a God—at least she guessed she did—but she never felt that kind of connection everyone else talked about feeling with Him. It just wasn't right for her.

"Well, I'm glad you have such a good outlook on it, Brantley."

Brantley was looking out onto the ocean. "Hey, the way I have learned to see it, they never belonged to me. God allowed me to have them as amazing parents for nine years, but ultimately, they belonged to Him. It was His right to take them home when He was ready for them. I finally understand that."

"You seem to be a really strong Christian?" Lyndie asked, not really meaning it to come out like a question but more of a statement.

"My grandparents always made sure I was in church. I just dug deeper in my walk with God, learning more of Who He is and Who He wants me to be. That's really all it is. I have a very good Friend and Father, and He also happens to be God. It's kind of cool."

Lyndie smiled at that. Normally when people talked like that, she thought it was cheesy; but for some reason, when Brantley said it, it sounded so natural and confident—like he really meant it.

"What about you? We live in the Bible Belt, so I know you either grew up in church or at least attended Vacation Bible School every summer."

Lyndie felt her skin crawl. She was never comfortable when asked about her own faith.

"Well, I grew up in church. Actually, my dad serves as a deacon at my home church. I guess I just never really felt that connection everyone else always talked about. I believe in God; I just feel like I am so busy, it's hard to find time to think about Him." A couple of seconds passed without him saying anything, so she interrupted the silence. "I know that probably sounds horrible. I honestly have never told anyone that."

"No, I admire your honesty. Most girls would probably either have blown off the question altogether or lied about it. They'd never comment on their actual relationship with God."

She was surprised at his reaction and even more surprised that she had said that out loud. She wasn't used to having personal conversations with people her own age, much less those she had just met, about God.

"Well, I guess there would be no use in feeding you what you want to hear. I'm not the best at making up stories."

He smiled her way. "I think God has you on a journey. You'll understand with time. He's got something up His sleeve." She didn't know how to respond to that. He must have sensed that and continued, "I mean, He is constantly pursuing you. Maybe before long, you'll have to make time for Him, in a good way." They walked a bit more and casually turned back toward where they had come. The band was off the stage, and people had already mostly cleared out.

"So what was it like growing up here? It must have been amazing."

Brantley let out a chuckle. "I guess since I grew up here, I didn't think much of it. I loved it—don't get me wrong—but when I was younger, I honestly thought everyone lived at a beach. It was a very relaxed and playful childhood. I was always outside, even in the winter."

"I can't even imagine. This has always been a vacation spot for me, so it's hard for me to process that people do actually live here."

They walked a bit longer and let the silence fall between them— it felt comfortable, strangely enough. They reached the pier that led back to Lyndie's hotel.

"Well, would you like me to walk you to your hotel? Normally, this place isn't dangerous at night, but all y'all raging college kids seem to turn it upside down," he said playfully.

Lyndie laughed lightly, and though she liked the idea, she decided that she should probably go ahead by herself. "I appreciate that, but since I did just take a long walk on the beach with a stranger, I'm feeling a little rebellious tonight. I should be fine."

Brantley gave a polite nod. "Back home safe and sound."

"I am glad I met you today. I really enjoyed myself," Lyndie said, trying to figure out how to say goodbye.

"Me, too. I guess I will see you tomorrow."

She wasn't so sure what he meant, so he added, "I am your captain on the boat, remember? To take y'all back?"

Duh, she thought to herself. "Oh right, I will see you then. Have a good rest of your night." Lyndie smiled at him and began to walk away, that same excited feeling in the pit of her stomach.

"Goodnight, be safe!" Brantley called after her, and she could feel him watching as she turned away and started up to her hotel room. Suddenly, he called after her, "Lyndie!"

She turned around, looking surprised. What was he going to ask?

"I don't know if y'all have plans in the morning, but if you're free, I have this place I go in the mornings from time to time. If you'd like, I'd love to take you there."

Lyndie felt her stomach do flip flops. "I think that would be okay. Promise you're a sane person?"

"You'll have to trust me, but I promise." He smiled.

"Okay, then you wanna meet here in the morning?"

"Yep; is six o'clock too early?"

"I can handle that, but it better be pretty."

"I promise it's worth it."

She smiled. "I'll see you then."

He watched again as she walked up towards the hotel. She thought to herself, *I just planned a date with a guy I don't even know. What was I thinking? Why was she so excited about it?* He obviously wasn't like any guy she'd ever met.

As she neared the room, she could hear loud music coming from down the hall.

Their hotel room was empty with a note in Jodie's handwriting, saying: "Lyndie—down the hall at Brett and Case's room—they are throwing a party—come over if ya want. Love ya."

Lyndie almost felt relieved; she just wanted to be alone. She changed into her pajamas and tucked herself in her bed, thoughts running through her mind replaying the night and everything she and Brantley had discussed. How was she ever going to fall asleep?

12

Brantley

Brantley woke up at 5:30 buzzing with excitement. He quickly took a shower, drank his coffee, and threw on his board shorts and an old t-shirt. He got to the boat at about 5:50 and reminded himself he only had about ten minutes to get his boat ready. At six o'clock on the dot, he saw Lyndie walking down toward the sand where he had said goodbye to her the night before. Seeing her in the glimmer of sunshine that was peeking through the clouds reminded him of how beautiful she was.

"Pleased to see you showed up."

Lyndie laughed softly. "Well, of course. I gotta keep my word."

He smiled at that. "Well, I will be your captain for the day, madam. If you would just follow me aboard the ship, I will be happy to show you where we are sailing to today."

13

Lyndie

His joking quickly eased Lyndie's nerves. She let out a breath to herself and smiled.

"Okay, Gilligan, sounds good to me." They made their way onto the boat. Lyndie followed him to the top deck, where she wasn't allowed just a day earlier.

"You are welcome to sit on that chair there; it's the mate's chair. Oh, and here's a blanket if you get cold—I thought the breeze might be a little chilly." Lyndie made herself comfortable in the chair and draped the blanket over her legs. As Brantley got the boat started, she looked out over the horizon. The ocean was so calm, and the sun was beginning to peek through the sky. She felt fresh and a sense of bliss. He still hadn't told her where they were going, but she figured she'd let it be a surprise. She was in awe as a beautiful island with an old lighthouse appeared on the horizon. Even though to most, the lighthouse would seem eerie, it was the most perfect sight she had ever seen. The beach curved into a tight circle along the ocean shore, and palm trees lined the island as if everything was hand-placed exactly where it was.

"Wow, how did you find this? It's incredible," she said in almost a whisper.

Brantley let a smile of satisfaction spread across his face. "When I was younger, my parents would sail us here, and we would spend all day with friends and family grilling out and playing music. Those were some of my best memories." He went on, "I have no idea how they found it, but whoever would come to the island with us had to always promise they'd only share it with people they saw as special."

Lyndie could feel her cheeks getting warm. "So I guess I'm special?"

"I may be jumping the gun, but from the moment I met you, something told me you were." He sounded so smooth and confident when he said it, but genuine all the same. "Hang on one sec and let me dock the boat—then we'll go explore. The sun is starting to rise over the horizon so you can go ahead and get on the island if you'd like."

Lyndie made her way down off the giant boat and let her toes squish in the sand as she stepped onto the island. The sand was fresh and clean, as if no one had ever stepped foot on it before. She saw a piece of driftwood on the sand that she decided to sit on as she waited on Brantley. The sun was rising, and she could hardly believe her eyes. It was beautiful with blazing orange, red, and yellow colors spread across the sky.

"Looks like Heaven's coming down to meet us, huh?" Brantley said as he took a seat beside her. He had a thermos of coffee in his hand and two mugs. "You like coffee? I only drink it sometimes, but this morning, it seemed appropriate—it's hard to watch the sunrise without a cup of coffee in your hands."

Lyndie gave him a child-like grin. "You think of everything don't you?"

Brantley smiled sheepishly and poured her a mug.

They watched the sunrise in silence for a while—it wasn't weird or uncomfortable; to Lyndie, it felt strangely natural. Lyndie eventually broke the silence. "Does it get any easier, you know, missing your parents?"

Brantley looked down at his mug, then looked her in the eyes. "It does, and it doesn't. It's harder because I'm getting older, and the older I get, the more stuff I remember they won't be here for, like when I graduate or when I get married. Then in a strange way, it also gets easier, just not in the way you would think. With every passing day, I usually think how this is one day closer to getting to see them again, and it makes me all the more excited."

"Can I ask what happened to them?"

"They had gone out early one morning to free-dive off my dad's boat in the middle of the ocean. No one had begun to realize they'd been gone longer than usual until later that evening. I was at my grandparents and hadn't thought much of it. Then I could tell my grandparents had started to get worried that they weren't back. So they got a neighbor to come watch me and stayed gone late into the night. Even though I was still young, I knew something wasn't right. I prayed and prayed that nothing was wrong with my parents. When my grandparents got home that night, they told me not to worry, but I could see in their eyes that they were worried themselves. I remember that to always be the worst night of my life. Not knowing what was going on, where they were—it was a panic I had never felt before." He paused for a second and went on. "The next day, they sat me down. My grandma pulled me in close, and with tears in his eyes, my papa broke the news to me that my parents' boat had been found empty about two miles from where they had been diving. My parents weren't in it. Although they promised they would continue to search, there was a good chance something went wrong. It could have been a number of things, but they never could find them."

"I can't imagine how hard that would be. I am so sorry, Brantley," were the only words she could find to say.

"Like I said, if I didn't have that hope that I would see them again, I would be a wreck; but because of that, I have made peace."

"That is good you are so optimistic about everything."

"What, don't you get excited when you think of getting to see the people you love again after they die?"

"I don't think of it like that. I guess I have a really hard time thinking of Heaven as a realistic place. When my grandpa passed away, I just felt like we said our goodbyes. I never really meditated on the fact that I could see him again one day."

"Yeah, Heaven is still hard for me to wrap my mind around, too. It is for everyone, I believe, but I have to pray to God about it. I feel like the closer I get to Him, the closer I get to understanding Heaven."

"That's all really confusing for me, though. It sounds so much simpler when someone else is talking about it, but then when I try to pray or something, I get insecure or get distracted. I guess it's just me. I don't know."

Seeming to sense her insecurity on the subject, Brantley simply said, "It's okay to have doubts; we all have those." The way he said it wasn't judgmental or like he was condemning her.

"Yeah, I mean, I believe something had to create us, but I guess God seems far-fetched, too. I almost dislike thinking about it, and I really hate thinking about dying. The thought scares me so much."

"Don't get me wrong," Brantley said hesitantly. "I certainly have my off-days when I just can't pray to God, when I feel as if He doesn't care or I am just angry with Him because life hasn't gone the way I want it to. Can I suggest something?" "Sure," Lyndie replied.

"Just try every night to pray, even if you feel awkward and you don't know what to say, and read your Bible. I feel like at some point, it will become a habit, and it may help how you are feeling."

"I guess it couldn't hurt," Lyndie agreed.

Brantley couldn't help but smile. "And if it works?"

"Then I'll say you were right."

"And I can take you out on another date?"

Her stomach fluttered. "When was the first one?"

Brantley gave her a soft smile and stared deep into her eyes. "What if I kissed you?"

"Are you asking if you can?"

"Maybe."

Before he could get a response out of her, she leaned in and kissed him softly. Then they both beamed like they were kids and it was their first kiss. Brantley noticed it was complete daylight and checked the time on his watch. "I better be getting you back to your friends before they start worrying."

"Please, they are both probably off drooling over guys on the beach right now or still asleep. But you're right; I probably do need to get back soon."

He helped her back up on the boat, and they sailed back across the water to Folly. Once they arrived, Brantley docked the boat and led her back down.

He embraced her in a gentle hug, "I've loved getting to know you the past couple of hours, Lyndie. I hope I will see you again soon."

Lyndie looked up at him. "Well, you are sailing us back," she said with a giggle.

"Well, I guess for once, I'll be looking forward to work then." She told him she'd see him later and then made her way back to the hotel. He watched as she walked back across the beach.

Lyndie spent Saturday evening with her friends. They met up with some other people from the sorority for a low country boil and sat around a fire on the beach. Just like every other time, everyone was having way too much to drink. All throughout the night, her friends kept asking what was bugging her, but Lyndie couldn't help but feel distant. She was even able to ignore the guys' catcalls. Her mind felt like it was a million miles away, or a couple of hours away, down the street. She couldn't help but look for him everywhere—every time she saw a guy with hair like his, her heart would flutter. Eventually, she told Jodie and Rachael she was turning in early and walked alone up to their room. She tried packing her stuff up for the next morning, but she soon got frustrated by how she was feeling and eventually threw herself in bed. She laid there for what seemed like ten hours with her eyes wide open. What was he doing right now? Was he thinking of her, too? Surely not. But then again, goodness, how she wished he was. Was she crazy for feeling so strongly for a guy after knowing him for two days? Those things only happened in the movies, right? And then there was that nagging thought about all their conversations about God. She couldn't ignore the fact that they had sparked interest and feelings of guilt. She remembered that she had told him she would try to pray and read her Bible even when it wasn't easy to do. She felt silly as she said in almost a whisper, "God if you're out there and listening, I probably have disappointed You, and I'm sorry. If so, I don't know what to say, so just know I'm trying or I'm going to. Amen."

14

Brantley

About two miles down the road, Brantley was sitting on his buddy's back deck playing guitar with his friends. They did this a good bit. He kept wanting to bring up Lyndie to his friends, but he knew if he did, he would probably never hear the end of it. After he couldn't take it any longer, he let the words, "I met a girl," slip right off of his lips. The biggest childlike grin spread across his face.

"I bet I know where you met this girl," Chip said.

"The one from the boat the other day?" Matt butted in. Everyone was immediately interested. They weren't used to Brantley meeting girls that he actually liked, much less any he would talk to them about.

"I don't know, y'all. She's authentic, and I guess I've only known her for two days so I probably shouldn't be bringing her up so soon, but she's different from anyone I've ever met."

"Huh. I've said that before," their friend Zain butted in. Brantley ignored the comment.

"That's great, man, but if she's anything like her friends, don't you think she's a little bit wild for your taste?" Matt asked.

"That's the thing; she's not at all like that—she is honestly a lot like me. I think she has some difficulties understanding God, though, but don't we all?"

Chip looked concerned. "What do you mean?"

"I don't know, I don't wanna go into a lot of details because it's her business, not any of ours." Brantley decided to leave it at that.

15

Lyndie

Lyndie woke up the next morning feeling nervous. She felt like she was in high school again, about to see her crush. The girls were fishing all morning for clues of how yesterday went with Brantley. Surprisingly, Lyndie didn't feel like talking about it with them, even though she was used to telling them everything. After they ate breakfast together and packed, they headed down to the boat dock. A lot of people had left the day before, so thankfully, it wasn't nearly as crowded. She heard church bells in the distance and thought about how Brantley was probably going to be coming straight from church. He had briefly told her on the way back to Folly yesterday about the church he attended, and he talked about the people who attended there like they were family. She thought about how long it had been since she had last been to church. And then as soon as the thought popped up, she tried to push it away, but it only made her feel even worse. No matter how excited she was to see Brantley again, the nagging feeling that something in her life wasn't quite right was still there, and it was putting her in the worst of moods. Suddenly, she felt a hand gently touch her shoulder. She turned around but already knew who it was.

"Hey, stranger," Brantley said with a smile.

"Hey yourself. You were almost late, and then you would have had a bunch of hungover, angry college kids to deal with."

"They couldn't have been too mad after I explained I was late because I was at church. We are still in the Bible Belt, ya know."

Lyndie laughed lightly.

Jodie jumped in and shook Brantley's hand like he was in for a job interview.

"I'm Jodie, and this is Rachael. We never got to formally meet. Sorry about all that the other day, by the way."

"Nice to officially meet you. Lyndie's told me . . . great things about y'all."

"Well, I'm glad she's talkative with you. We can't get anything out of her about you," Rachael said with a sly grin, flashing eyes at Lyndie.

Brantley laughed casually. "Well, sorry to have to run out, but duty calls. I'll see y'all on the boat. Let me know if y'all have any problems."

As he turned to make his way through the line to open up the boat, he glanced back at Lyndie and flashed that sweet smile she was already admiring. Once they all were allowed to board the boat, Brantley found her and asked if she wanted to sit up top with him. As much as she wanted to, she felt guilty because she had hardly spent any time with Rachael and Jodie all weekend. She told him she would love to, but she felt like she should stay down there with her friends and that she would find him after they docked. The whole ride back, though, she was wishing she was up there with him. Occasionally, she would sneak a peek up at the captain's seat at him, and most of the time when she did, he would catch her eye, too. Every time, it gave her butterflies.

Once they arrived, everyone had begun to pile out of the boat. When she stayed behind, Rachel and Jodie caught on and said they'd go to the t-shirt shop at the marina and look around until she was done.

Their eyes met, and she couldn't stop grinning. "I'll have to say, I sorta missed ya up there," Brantley said.

"I can't say I loved being down here—your driving about made me seasick," she said sarcastically.

"Hey, that's what you get for not coming up there with me. So, when am I gonna see you again?"

"Well, classes start back this week, which I guess you know already, so honestly I am not too sure what my schedule will look like. I'll give you my number, and you can let me know when is best for you."

"Sounds good to me. If you'd like, I wouldn't mind taking you out for dinner in the city one night or grabbing coffee between classes because I really have enjoyed spending time with you. I think we are on to a great friendship," he said with a nudge. She didn't know exactly how to take that comment.

"Me, too. Thanks for hanging out with me this weekend and for, well, keeping me sane."

"It was my pleasure," Brantley assured her.

Silence fell between them. "Well, I guess I better get going. Again, thanks for everything, and hopefully, I will see you again soon," Lyndie said, not knowing if she should hug him or just walk away.

"You will."

As if Brantley was reading her mind, he embraced her in a hug, then pulled away. "Bye, Lyndie. We'll talk soon." She forced herself to walk away and could feel herself blushing. Boy, did she have some thinking to do.

16
Brantley

A week passed by without Brantley calling her. He didn't want to come off too eager, and he had been very busy with classes starting. He knew she would be, too. After the second day, he decided he'd give her a call and ask if she wanted to hang out with him. He wasn't one to go out into Charleston for fancy dinners—he hardly spent any time in the city of Charleston unless it involved school or he absolutely had to. Because of that, he really didn't know where he would even take her. That is, if she even agreed to hang out with him again. He got up and decided to ask the one person he could always count on to tell him the right thing to do.

"Hey, Grandma, you got any ideas for me about nice places to take a girl to in Charleston?"

She perked up like a flower. "Well, of course. Who is this young girl?"

"Just somebody I met over the weekend. She's very nice; you'll like her."

"Well, of course, I will soon. You've got a good head on your shoulders. I'd like any girl you bring home. Hmm, now let me think. I know! Take her to the place where me and your granddaddy had our first date, Magnolia's in Charleston. It's been there for ages, and it's wonderful. It's good for anytime, too—brunch, lunch, or dinner." She went on. "Me and your grandaddy were both twenty years old when he took me there. I was so nervous, I could barely make conversation with him. We sat on a park bench talking for hours before he drove me home. He was truly a gentleman." She was smiling as if she was back sixty years ago on that same park bench with the love of her life.

Brantley liked the idea and thought it would be something Lyndie would like, too. She seemed like a simple girl, easy to please. After his classes that day, he decided to call her.

"Hello?"

"Hey, it's Brantley. How have you been?"

"Hey, Brantley, I've been good. I am a little overwhelmed because I started student teaching, and it's a lot more work than I expected, but it's okay. How've your classes been?"

She seemed to sound pleased to hear from him. He smiled with relief.

"Good for the most part—we are going out on the ocean sometime next week, so I'm pretty excited about that."

"Wow, that makes my classes *really* sound fun," she said with a laugh of sarcasm that he was already becoming familiar with.

"Ah, you have a fun job; it's what you love to do. So, um, I was actually calling to see what you were doing this weekend?"

"No plans yet. What did you have in mind?"

"Well, I wanted to see if you would like to have dinner with me at Magnolia's Saturday night?"

"That sounds great, actually. That's one of my favorite places to eat, but I haven't been in ages."

"Well, I'm glad I chose it then. I can pick you up at your apartment; some time around 5:30 p.m. work for you?"

"That'd be perfect! I can text you the address to my place."

"That works. I can't wait to see you, Lyndie." The way he said it surprised him. It even sounded confident to himself.

"I can't wait to see you, too! So you better not cancel if a last-minute fishing trip comes up." He knew she was joking with him, and it loosened him up a little.

"I would never, unless it was spearfishing—that's my favorite." He guessed she probably rolled her eyes and smiled when he said that.

"Yeah, yeah. Well, thank you for asking me; I'm walking into my classroom now, so I will talk to you soon."

Brantley laughed. "Have a good time in class. Bye, Lyndie." He hung up and felt like he had just won a million bucks.

17

Lyndie

Lyndie was relieved he had called her and asked her on a date. After a week of not hearing from him, she had begun to worry, but her friends kept reassuring her it was probably just that he was busy with school. She herself was busy and buried in schoolwork already.

The rest of the week dragged by as she awaited Saturday night. She loved Magnolia's but didn't particularly see Brantley eating there. He seemed like more of a beach bar-and-grill type of guy, but all the same, she was just happy she could spend some time with him. The girls piled in her room Saturday afternoon trying to help her decide which outfit to wear.

"Hmm, I say you go all out. He's never really seen you dressed up, ya know," Jodie suggested.

"Yeah, but they're going to Magnolia's; it's still not a suit and tie restaurant," Lyndie agreed with Rachael.

"How about this?" Lyndie held up a pastel purple dress that was cotton and flowed a little above her knees. She had strappy sandals and a long, gold necklace to go with it.

"That's perfect!" they all agreed. Lyndie didn't typically wear a lot of makeup, but she put on a little eyeshadow, powder, and mascara and blew out her hair. She checked the time. It was 5:20—he would be there any minute.

As soon as she thought this, she heard the girls hollering, "He's here, Lyndie!" Her whole body shook nervously. She didn't like not feeling sure of herself like this. She made her way to the door, and there he stood, clean as a whistle in a light blue polo shirt, khaki shorts, and leather flip flops. He sure was a sight.

"You look great, Lyndie," he said as he brought her in for a hug. She blushed.

"Y'all have fun. Don't have her home too late!" Rachael called after them as they walked out of the door. They talked easily to one another on the way to Magnolia's, mostly about school and all the work they were taking on from it. Once they found a parking spot and casually walked to the restaurant, both their stomachs were growling. A line was piling out of the restaurant. Lyndie didn't think about it being a Saturday night and how crowded it would be. They probably wouldn't eat for another two hours.

"We may have to go somewhere else, especially if you are as hungry as I am," Lyndie said with a sweet smile.

"I got reservations; we Folly boys can be fancy every now and again," he said with a wink. "Well, and we have good grandparents who remind us we may want to make a reservation." Lyndie laughed. She was so impressed with everything he did. The two of them walked up to the host stand.

"Hey. I have a reservation for two—it's under Barns," Brantley told the woman.

"Well, now, at least I know your last name."

He smiled back at her as they made their way to their seats. "And what's yours?"

"Pruett."

"Well, it's good to meet you, Miss Pruett," he said as he scooted her chair out for her. They talked all through dinner, never missing a beat. Lyndie got she-crab soup, and he got deviled crab; both were surprised at how delicious it was. They talked about their childhood, their parents, their interests, and their friends. After the third time the waitress came to check on them, they realized that was probably their cue that she wanted them to get going.

Outside, Brantley took her hand easily and held it gently. "Would you want to go for a walk on the Battery?"

"That sounds great. I hardly ever come out here, and I love history, so it makes no sense," Lyndie said.

"If it makes you feel any better, I've lived right next to this beautiful city my whole life, and the only time I come is for school and work."

"Yeah . . . I'd say you need to get out more," Lyndie said with a laugh.

"I'll be honest, I didn't even know what Magnolia's was until my grandmother suggested I take you there; that's where she and my grandpa had their first date." She was flattered. "Well, tell your grandma she has excellent taste because that was great."

"Will do. She's already wanting to meet you—she's not used to me talking about girls with her."

Lyndie felt herself blush. "I'd love to meet her. She seems like an amazing woman." She meant that, too. The thought of meeting his grandparents didn't scare her; she wanted to know more about Brantley and his roots.

"Well, I know it's kind of last-minute, but tomorrow after church, we all have a big cookout—usually at my grandparents', since it's right next to the water—and we surf, paddleboard, play cornhole, and all the friends in the neighborhood come out. You should come." Lyndie knew she didn't have any plans—Jodie and Rachael usually slept all day on Sundays.

"That sounds great! But I have to tell you, I cannot surf to save my life."

"But I bet you've never had a teacher like me." Brantley laughed.

"Seriously, don't expect much. I have no hand-eye coordination at all, but I'll give it a try. What church do you go to?"

"Folly Baptist. Surprisingly, though, it's not all that traditional. Most people walk to it from their houses, and a lot of times, we have service on the beach. We play Contemporary Christian music; and Jack, our preacher, speaks with so much passion, it's hard to even let your mind drift during service. I've gone there my whole life, and I love it."

"That sounds nice. I've been trying to keep my word to you about praying and reading my Bible. Well, not a whole lot of my Bible because I can't find it, honestly, but I have been praying. It gets easier, but I don't know if it's still uncomfortable."

"It may be like that for a while—it is for everyone—but once you understand Who God is, it gets less awkward." He paused. "Uh, would you like to come to church with me tomorrow?"

She hesitated before answering. "Well, I guess it wouldn't hurt. My parents would be over the moon if I told them I met a guy who took me to church. What time?"

"Be there around nine o'clock. I can wait for you at the door. Are you sure you don't want me to come and pick you up?" Brantley asked. He truly was a gentleman.

"No, I want to drive. I hardly ever get to drive places since I mostly walk everywhere."

"Well, I'm glad you're coming." He smiled as if he truly meant it. They walked along the sidewalk overlooking the bay where the moon reflected off the water. It felt wonderful outside with fall making its way through. Lyndie was completely relaxed. She was thankful Brantley wasn't pushing the God subject. She needed time to think and meditate on all she was feeling because she felt like he had opened up a book within her that had been closed for so long now. She was so conflicted and felt that neediness that nothing was providing for her.

"You okay?" Brantley asked her as he gently squeezed her hand.

"Yes, just lost in thought. It's so beautiful out here tonight."

"I was thinking the same thing. It's amazing how much history this place holds. Hundreds of years ago, men who we read about in our history books walked where we are walking and fought to defend our home. It's an incredible thought."

"It is, and so many people take it for granted. We come to Charleston for the beach and the shops and the charm, and we forget how much knowledge it holds, how it's seen far more than we could ever imagine."

"Exactly. Sadly, I feel as if our generation doesn't think that way anymore or care. I know I even have to remind myself sometimes." She loved his honesty; she wasn't used to that in men. They stopped and looked off at the water. He turned to her. "I am so happy I met you; I really do feel like it was for an important reason, Lyndie." He smiled at her.

"I do, too," she said. He gently kissed her, long and sweet. They stopped for ice cream on the way back to the car, and when he pulled in front of her apartment, she couldn't help but feel disappointment. She didn't want the night to end.

"I'm so happy I'm gonna get to see you in the morning," she said.

"Me, too. Thank you for everything tonight. It really was perfect." He did that sideways grin at her. He got out and came to her side to open the door. No guy had ever done that for her. She got out and looked up at him. His gray eyes were glistening.

"Get some sleep. I'll see you in the a.m.," he said and kissed her again. She could definitely get used to that.

"Drive safe, Brantley. Thank you again." He waited for her to go inside before he drove off. She felt like she was on cloud nine as she made her way to get ready for bed.

Lyndie made the beautiful drive to Folly Beach early the next morning. She was nervous. The last time she had been to church was when she was around sixteen years old. She let herself remember what it had been like growing up going to youth group, all the Vacation Bible Schools, and the lock-ins. She missed those easier days. Every Wednesday while in school, she could hardly concentrate on her schoolwork because her mind would be thinking about going to youth group that night. So much had gone wrong. Her parents still attended church on Sundays and were avidly involved, and she hated that they would never be able to understand why she stopped going. It had been so long. She believed God was real, but it didn't come easy to her to have a relationship with Him like it seemed to other people.

She honestly was surprised Brantley was even interested in her because they were so different. He needed someone who had the same strong faith as he did. She never made herself vulnerable like she was now, and the last thing she needed was her heart broken. She made herself stop thinking so negatively; it was getting her nowhere. She crossed the bridge to Folly that overlooked the marsh. It was so beautiful here, and, like always, she wondered why she didn't make her way over to Folly more. It was one of the main reasons she had chosen the College of Charleston in the first place.

She was about to turn down Main Street when she saw the church on her right. She remembered noticing it before because it was so charming. She caught herself mentally rehearsing what to say to people when they introduced themselves, and then she told herself that was ridiculous—she was who she was, and there was no need to worry about impressing people.

Like Brantley had promised, he was standing on the top step of the church. He saw her as soon as she turned in the parking lot. She found a spot and walked over to him. He looked more casual than she had expected. His hair was pulled back, and he had a soft, gray shirt, khaki pants, and flip flops. She started to feel overdressed in her sundress until she looked around and noticed all the other women in dresses.

"Hey, you look wonderful," he said as he wrapped her in a sweet hug.

"You look pretty nice yourself. I've passed this church before; it's cute," she said as they walked in.

"Yeah. I love it; it's kinda like my second home; and, uh, just a heads up, people are probably going to introduce themselves to you left and right." As soon as he said this, a sweet-looking older lady who looked to be in her mid-seventies approached them.

"You must be Lyndie. I'm Jean, Brantley's grandmother." Before she could even respond, Jean had wrapped her up in a big bear hug.

When she pulled away, Lyndie replied, "It's great to meet you. I have heard so much about you." Jean gave Brantley a joking smile, which Lyndie noted was the same grin he gave her all the time.

"Better be good things—you never know with this one." Her accent was thick like a Southern debutante.

The inside was just as quaint as the outside. There were shiny, white, wooden pews and big, stained glass windows made from blue and green sea glass. It helped her relax a little.

"Well, I have to go join the choir. Brantley, would y'all like to sit with me and your pa?" she called as she started to walk towards the stage.

"Sure, Grandma!" Brantley took Lyndie around and introduced her to as many people as possible on the way to their seats. They piled into the pew next to a tall man with dark skin and hair that Lyndie could tell was turning from salt-and-pepper to white. She knew immediately that had to be Brantley's pa. He stood up to greet them, a smile spreading across his face.

"Well, this must be the young lady you've paid to pretend to be your girlfriend."

"Yep. Pa, this is her. Now, don't blow her cover." Brantley laughed. Lyndie could tell he was completely in his comfort zone.

"I'm Lyndie. It's great to finally meet you."

Pa reached over and hugged her. "It's great to meet you, too, sweetheart. Anyone who can keep our Brantley in line is always someone great to meet," he said as he grabbed Brantley's shoulder.

The preacher came onstage and asked everyone to have a seat. That was their cue. Lyndie tried to make herself comfortable on the pews. As the pastor talked, she found herself glancing around at all the new faces. Everyone she had met was so friendly, and she wished she wasn't so on-edge at the moment. Brantley took her hand and gently squeezed it. She looked up at him, and he gave her a sideways smile. It warmed her heart, and she tried to remind herself why she was there. But deep down, she knew it wasn't just for Brantley. Although he had stirred these thoughts she had pushed down a long time ago, she was here to figure out some of her own answers and struggles. She had no idea where to begin, but she told herself church would probably be the best place to start.

The choir sang one hymn she remembered from when she was little. Although she didn't sing it out loud, her heart remembered the words: "Precious Lord take my hand, Lead me on, Let me stand, I am tired, I am weak, I am worn. Through the storm, through the night, Lead me on to the light . . . "

After that, they sang more praise and worship songs. Since her church growing up didn't play much contemporary music, she didn't know the words, but she still hummed along. After the music was over, the preacher came on. He looked to be in his early fifties and had a kind face. He welcomed everyone and went over a few announcements, and then his face got serious. He smiled faintly.

"How strong are those words, 'Precious Lord take my hand, Lead me on to the light'? I am far from knowing everything there is to know about this world, Jesus, the Bible, and Heaven. Some days, I wake up just as confused as the next person about what Heaven will be like or how it is that the God of this universe can still have conversations all throughout the day with me, a lowly preacher man, who grew up in a small town in South Carolina. How did I deserve that? My mind can't wrap around the fact that I will get to live for eternity without end. Try as I might, I simply cannot figure these things that we all have questions about. But then, there are times, like that time I sang that song at my mother's graveside, where I've felt infinite peace, peace that surpasses all, that brings me back to my Father's feet. I remember He's living' He's waiting for us with open arms.

"The truth is, we don't have to understand it all; we just have to understand His love for us. A forgiving, perfect love. In those times that we are tired of living, we are confused and don't know what to do to replace that empty, achy feeling in our hearts. He is right there to guide us on to the light. Because, Folks, He *is* the Light. He has been there all along, waiting for us to just reach out for him and let him take our hands. That is the only way we will feel whole. This life will leave us scarred and empty. He fills us up; He leads us to greener pastures and loves us like nothing else can. We don't deserve love like this, but He gives it freely. Friends, I felt like I needed to let my heart come through and to say that. I know some of you may be going through confusion, not understanding or feeling God. He's there, though. Seek and you will find. Don't give up because He won't ever give up on you."

Lyndie felt cold chills rush through her body. All she could think was, *Did Brantley tell him about me?* But when she looked over at Brantley, he looked like he was completely in his own world. He wouldn't have done that. There had to be some explanation.

She couldn't help but ask in the back of her mind, *Was that God trying to get my attention?* This kind of stuff didn't happen to her. But despite all her confusion, what he said touched her heart. It seemed to have hope tied to it, and she felt awakened and confused all at the same time. She needed to talk with someone about this. She just didn't know who. The preacher continued for another twenty minutes and then called for anyone who wanted to come pray or talk to him to come up to the front. Every nerve in her body was telling her to move. She didn't know why, but her feet stayed planted. She didn't go forward; she stayed there with those thoughts buzzing through her mind.

18

Brantley

Brantley was surprised himself at how Preacher Bill's message seemed to be directed right toward Lyndie. After the service, Brantley and Lyndie had lunch with his grandparents at their home. He watched her out of the corner of his eye as the breeze from the sea blew her hair as they sat on the screened-in porch. Brantley could tell her mind was a million miles away. He put his hand on top of hers and gave her a slight smile, giving her the space he felt that she needed.

19

Lyndie

When Brantley had to go help his grandpa with something, she decided to go chat with his grandma Jean. "Hey, Mrs. Jean, do you need help with anything? It smells wonderful in here."

"Oh, honey just call me Jean. And, well, if you could fill up four glasses of tea, that would be wonderful; you like sweet tea, right?"

"Yes, ma'am. So what is on the menu?" Lyndie asked.

"Shrimp and grits, sweet tea, key lime pie for dessert. This has always been my favorite meal; the guys get tired of it, so I have to wait for special occasions to cook it now."

"Well, shrimp and grits is one of my favorites."

They made small talk as they fixed the meal. Lyndie really liked Jean and found it easy to connect with her. The meal was delicious, and she enjoyed Brantley and his family's company. After dinner, Brantley helped his papa with something on his car outside while she and Jean drank coffee on the porch.

"So Brantley tells me you are going to school to be an art teacher," Jean said.

"Yeah, I always loved art in school but had a hard time in other classes. Art was always my best subject."

"I've always loved art, too. I try to paint sometimes, but I'm definitely no Picasso," Jean said with a chuckle.

"That's the great thing about art, though—you don't have to be good to enjoy it. It's always been my personal therapy."

"I can see that. It's kind of like when I read my Bible or pray. That's my therapy."

Lyndie hesitated. "Yeah, that used to be mine when I was young, too, but I've found it difficult these past years."

"Oh, we all go through those times when it's hard to pray. You will get back to it; you just have to keep trying."

"Well, you see, I let myself drift out of church when I went to college. It's not exactly been something I've done for a while," said Lyndie.

Jean laid her hand on Lyndie's. "You're not the first, and you won't be the last. Whatever doubts you're having about Him, He's there. He understands."

Lyndie felt oddly comfortable. She liked talking to Jean, and she could tell where Brantley got his easy-going personality. She spent a little while longer there and then, as the sun was starting to set, decided it was time to head back. She hugged Brantley's grandparents goodbye, and Brantley walked her to her car. She felt his fingers thread through her own, as if it was perfectly natural. They caught each other's eyes, and Lyndie began to feel as if he was becoming a part of her and her life so quickly. She had never fallen for anyone this fast and this much, but she couldn't help it, nor did she want to. He looked down at her and kissed the brim of her nose.

"Thank you for coming. My family adores you."

"It was a great day. I really enjoyed being around them—and you, of course," she said with a flirty smile.

He pulled her in for a hug. "Lyndie, you're quite the woman." She held on tight to him, feeling as though this was only temporary, for some reason. He pulled back a little and looked at her. "I want you on the road before it gets dark. Drive safe and let me know when you get home."

"Yes, sir. I'll be extra safe just for you," she said as she kissed him on the cheek. He let his hand graze her cheekbone and tilted her head up to kiss her softly.

The whole way home, she could not stop thinking about him and how he made her feel. A man had never made her feel valuable and beautiful like Brantley did. Almost as soon as she made it into her apartment, she called him, and they talked for two hours straight, never missing a beat.

When she got off the phone, she fell asleep easily but was awakened from a bad dream. She was alone on a boat in the middle of the ocean with a storm coming her way. She could see Brantley and her friends and family on land in the distance but couldn't get to them. She cried and cried, but nothing could get their attention. As she saw the rain like a curtain drifting its way toward her, she felt someone pick her up and swim her over to an island nearby with a canopy. She didn't feel panic when she felt the stranger pick her up; she felt safe and at peace. Then she heard the stranger say, "I am with you always; no one can love you more than I." And he disappeared. That's when she woke up. The dream stayed on her mind all day, and she told no one but Brantley about it. He told her it sounded like God might be trying to tell her something. She wasn't sure what to make of that.

20

Brantley

The following weeks passed easily as fall began to set in. Brantley spent most of his days working and going to school and spent any free time with Lyndie. Not only was he falling hard for her, but she was also becoming his best friend. It felt so natural being around her and calling her every day as they found out more about each other. They talked about everything—from their dreams, fears, and their childhoods. He was starting to notice her interest in growing closer to God again, but he didn't want to push her, nor for her to think the only reason he was pursuing her was to change her. He knew only God could do that. He simply wanted to be with her and to spend time getting to know her even more. It was Friday, and he was finishing up his shift at the marina and driving down with her to Clemson for the weekend to meet her family. For some reason, he wasn't nervous. He was actually looking forward to meeting the parents who raised the woman he was falling so passionately for. Work seemed to creep by as he waited for 3:30 p.m. to finally come. He kept checking his phone until the time finally came to clock out and meet Lyndie. He called her as soon as he got in his truck.

She answered on the second ring. "Well, hello there."

He smiled to himself. "Hey, darling, I'm finally off; that seemed like the longest work shift ever."

"Ah, but it's over now. Are you nervous yet?"

"Should I be?" he replied.

She snickered to herself. "Well, most guys are when they are meeting the parents, but you can be an exception to that rule. I don't mind."

"I am really just excited to meet them; they are a big part of your life, and I find it interesting to see where you came from."

"Well, don't be expecting too much; we really aren't all that interesting."

"I doubt that—you are one of the most interesting people I know. But then again, I might be a little biased." He could almost picture her smiling on the other side of the phone, the way he caught himself doing most all the time now.

"I love when you say stuff like that. Now when you gonna get yourself over here?"

"I'm on my way now. I brought my stuff with me so I could come straight there." They talked almost until he was at her apartment. When he got there, he embraced her in a big hug. He breathed in the already-familiar scent of her hair that always smelled tropical and warm to him. He helped her get her stuff into his truck.

The ride there shifted between silence as they listened to whatever song Lyndie played and chatting about her family and what he should expect. They stopped at a Cracker Barrel on the way. It was his first time ever going to one, and she promised he'd love it, which, surprisingly, he did. They came into the Upstate around 8:30 p.m. He remembered going there as a kid in the summers. Sometimes, his family would take day trips to go hiking at Table Rock or go on the Parkway; and a couple of times, they would spend weekends there camping on the Eastatoee River or on Lake Hartwell. However, it had changed a lot, even since he was a kid. It had become much more developed than he remembered. As they were coming out of Greenville, he took in the sights of places he recalled as woods in his childhood that were now shopping stores and restaurants. It definitely seemed like there was a lot more to do now than there used to be.

Thirty minutes later, they came into the outskirts of Clemson. They rode through Main Street of the town she lived in, lined with white farmhouses, antique shops, and cafés—this was the Upstate he remembered.

"This is Six Mile, where I grew up. The university is about fifteen minutes away," she said. He could hear the trace of pride in her voice, the kind of pride that comes only from someone who grew up in a small town like this one. He knew it well because it was the same kind of pride he felt about Folly.

"I love it; it's very charming."

They turned into her driveway, which was rather long and snaked along a huge front yard. The house was average-sized but looked very well-kept and quaint. Her mom had fall decorations spilling onto the porch; and a big, fluffy, white dog was laying on the steps. He didn't even seem to bat an eye when they pulled up.

"I assume that's Hank," he said. She had already filled him in on the old dog she'd had since childhood.

"The one and only. I told you a burglar would break in, and he wouldn't even bark."

Her family came out onto the porch, all smiling from ear to ear. Brantley came around and opened her door for her.

"Hey, y'all!" Mrs. Pruett waved as she walked off the porch and embraced Lyndie in a big hug. Then she turned to him. "Brantley, it's so good to finally meet you. I'm Sher," she said as she pulled him into a hug.

"It's nice to meet you, Mrs. Sher. I'm so glad we're here."

"Oh, honey, you don't have to call me Missus. That's sweet of you, though. Good manners—I like that. I am so glad to have you here."

Lyndie rolled her eyes and laughed. By then, her dad had come onto the porch and was hugging her. It was easy to see how much they loved their daughter. He shook Brantley's hand and gave him a big pat on the back.

"Nice to meet you Brantley. I'm Mike."

"It's great to meet you. Y'all have a lovely home."

"Ah, that's all her; she loves decorating."

"Hmm . . . I'll remind you of that next time you complain because I've gone on a shopping spree for it," she said. He chuckled and kissed her on the cheek. Brantley took in how much Lyndie resembled her mother. With her dark features, the woman could probably pass for being in her thirties.

They went inside, and Lyndie showed Brantley to the guestroom, where he'd be staying. The house was warm and homey inside. The walls were lined with pictures of Lyndie and her brother. Lyndie had explained earlier that her brother was at an out-of-town basketball game but would be back tomorrow around lunchtime. They spent the next hour sitting and chatting in the den with her parents, mostly them asking him questions about his life and who he was. He found it interesting how open they were about their faith and how easy it was to talk with them about his own relationship with God.

At eleven o'clock, they all decided to turn in for the night. Lyndie's mom hugged them both goodnight and left Brantley and Lyndie to say their goodnights in private. He looked down at Lyndie, still amazed at how quickly his life had changed by her coming into it. He wrapped his arms around her and kissed the top of her head and then, lightly, her lips.

"I guess we should go to sleep. I know we are both beat after that drive." He could tell she was struggling to keep her eyes open, as he himself was, too.

"I'll miss you, but set your alarm for about 8:30. I want to sleep in a little later. You can just knock on my door to see if I am up."

"Okay sounds great to me—I wouldn't mind a couple extra minutes of sleep either."

She looked him deep in the eyes, and he couldn't help but think even with those pretty eyes glazed over from fighting sleep, she looked so beautiful. He couldn't imagine ever looking into anyone else's eyes. "You get you some sleep. Goodnight." He kissed her again, and they went into their separate rooms. Although he was tired, he couldn't help thinking about how she was in the room beside him fast asleep. He adored her like nobody else.

21

Lyndie

When Lyndie woke up the next morning, she had to remind herself that Brantley was in the other room. She heard her father and Brantley both talking in the living room. She smiled to herself—he sure wasn't shy. She would probably have laid in bed until she heard him get up if they were at his family's, but no, not Brantley. After she brushed her teeth and changed, she found her dad and Brantley sitting at the table drinking coffee while her mother fixed breakfast.

"Good morning, sleepyhead," Brantley said with a crooked grin. Her parents also welcomed her with a "good morning" and asked if she slept well. Her mom made a big breakfast for the four of them with eggs, pancakes, and bacon.

"So what's on the agenda today, Mom? I know you have to have something planned," Lyndie said over breakfast.

"Well, your brother is coming in at 12:30, and then I have a special day planned for us. I know you said Brantley loves animals, so I lined us up a trail ride at Eden Farms today; it's just outside of Table Rock, and it's the perfect day for it," she said with a proud smile. "I know he's used to sea animals. Have you ever been around horses, Brantley?"

"Other than the occasional pony rides at a festival, no, but I would love to go. I'm sure it will be fun."

After three attempts from her dad to back out and take Brantley fly fishing instead, the whole family was in agreement with her mom's plans. She had to admit she was excited herself—she hadn't ridden since she moved to Charleston. She used to love riding her friend's horses and always wanted one of her own.

Lyndie showed Brantley around Main Street and Clemson before meeting back up with her family at 12:30. Her brother, Chase, was there when they got back. She gave him a big hug. He was already taller than her. Her baby brother was growing up, no doubt. Chase took to Brantley almost immediately. At lunch, they carried the conversation while Lyndie and her parents listened and laughed.

22

Brantley

Brantley didn't know what to expect when they arrived at Eden Farms. It was a huge horse stable surrounded by pastures, woods, big barns, and arenas. He watched Lyndie's face light up as they got out of the car. She looked at him and smiled.

"Ya nervous?"

He laughed. "I'd be lying if I said I hadn't thought about all the things that could go wrong with me on a horse."

She grazed her hand across his back. "You'll be fine, and hey, you're not alone—Dad has hardly said a word on the way over here." *It was true,* he thought. At least he wasn't the only one who was new at this.

Their trail guide was a nice woman in her late thirties who seemed very experienced with horses. She gave them a short tour of the stables and showed them how to mount their horses. He got a little bit embarrassed when the lady had to help him up, but not anymore than Mike, who looked totally mortified. Once they were up on the saddle, they looked completely comfortable. They rode around in the ring for a while before they went on the trail. Brantley stayed behind Lyndie the entire time. She was totally in her element, and he loved watching how much fun she was having.

The trail was peaceful and relaxing. Since they had to walk in a single line, nobody was really talking, and it was the perfect time for Brantley to find himself alone with God. He prayed in his head, thanking God for the enormous blessing God had given him by putting Lyndie in his life. He prayed for her relationship and that God would use him to draw her closer to him. All too soon, the ride was over, and they were thanking their trail guide for the experience, promising to come back soon. After the ride and his conversation with God, Brantley had never felt so at peace.

They grilled out at Lyndie's parents' that night and sat around their fire pit roasting marshmallows. Brantley kept thinking to himself how perfect a day it was. At one point in the evening, Lyndie had looked at him as she wiped marshmallow off the corners of his mouth and noted that he "hadn't stopped smiling all day." He gave her a quick kiss and asked how he could stop with such a beautiful girl like her to enjoy it with, and he meant it.

The night ended with them playing a board game with her family when something strange happened. Mike asked if they were going to church with them tomorrow.

Lyndie quickly chimed in, "I think we are gonna try to get on the road as early as possible tomorrow to beat the traffic. Sorry, guys."

Lyndie's parents didn't look surprised but only gave each other sorrowful looks. Brantley didn't understand. Lyndie had said she really enjoyed going to church with him; he couldn't see why she wouldn't want to go to her home church with her family one Sunday. But he didn't push, and after the game was over, Lyndie quickly told everyone goodnight and even seemed in a hurry to tell Brantley goodnight, as if she was trying to avoid him. This left Brantley all the more confused. He knocked on her door after her parents had gone to sleep.

She cleared her throat then answered,

"Uh come in."

Brantley peeked his head in. She was sitting on the edge of the bed still in her clothes looking like something was weighing heavily on her mind.

"I just wanted to make sure you were okay; you acted kinda weird in there when your parents asked about church."

"I just really want to get back as soon as possible. I have a lot of school work I gotta finish before Monday."

Brantley wanted to push the issue, but instead decided to let it go. "Okay, no biggie."

She gave him a faint smile and said goodnight. Once Brantley was alone in bed, he started to think about why she was acting so strange. What had made the day be turned around so quickly? He decided to give Matt a call.

The phone rang twice before Matt picked up. "Hey, man, how's the fam?"

"They are pretty great. So far, the trip has been wonderful, but something's been on my mind."

"Uh oh, trouble in paradise?"

Brantley laughed. "Not exactly. I just feel like she is holding back a lot, especially any time I mention God. And tonight, her parents asked us to go to church with them tomorrow, and she almost look scared. And now she won't talk to me about it."

"Brantley, I know you want me to tell you what to do, but that's a complicated situation. Because you walk so closely with God, it's hard to imagine you being with someone who, well doesn't. But at the same time, we can't judge anyone else's walk with Him. You need to pray about it. If God wants you to pursue this girl, then things will work out. We all know how seriously you take who you're gonna marry—God sees your diligence in that."

They chatted a bit more and then got off the phone. Brantley thought about what Matt said until he fell asleep.

23

Lyndie

Lyndie barely slept that night. How was she going to be able to tell Brantley it wasn't just because she had drifted away from God that she didn't wanna go to church with her family? For years, she had been able to push away the memory of what happened and pretend like it never took place. She had moved on, moved away, and Brantley had gotten her back in church. Now she had to face what she never wanted to face. But she knew she had to if she wanted to be with Brantley. He would never understand why she didn't want to go to church. He had thought she was growing—and she was. She had been feeling closer than she had in years with God.

After hours of tossing and turning, she finally got out of bed and onto her knees. She closed her eyes and sat in silence for what seemed like an hour. Then she was surprised how easily the words began to spill out to God.

"God, I don't know what to do. I need to deal with this. I need to heal; but I am mortified, and I thought I was past it. You are the only other Person Who knows what happened, and You can give me strength to do whatever it is that I need to do. Please, God, give me peace."

She stopped as an idea suddenly washed over her. Was that truly the reason she grew apart from God? And could it be that she was blaming Him for what happened? She knew what she had to do—she would go tomorrow; she would face her fears; she would face the man she had spent the last five years trying to forget. She lay in bed and continued to pray, finally drifting off to sleep.

The next morning, she woke up before anyone else and knocked on Brantley's door. She heard a muffled voice say to come in; he must have been in a deep sleep.

"Sorry to wake you. I just wanted to let you know I changed my mind, and I'd like to go today if you still want to."

He smiled.

"Of course, that sounds great. What time do I need to start getting ready?"

"Probably in another hour. Thanks for being so patient with me."

She closed the door and went to the kitchen to make herself some coffee and tried to prepare herself for the day ahead. Her parents were completely surprised when she told them the news that they would be joining them. The whole time she was getting ready, she kept telling herself she needed to do this, and it would be a weight lifted off her shoulders. If she could just face her demons, she could have peace; and nobody else, especially Brantley, would have to find out. Brantley held her hand the whole way there and didn't say a whole lot, as if he knew something was still on her mind and she needed her own space to work through it.

Sycamore Baptist Church, a time capsule in Six Mile, looked exactly as she had remembered it. People were piling out of their cars in their best dress. She saw floods of familiar faces as they pulled in—some she felt a little excitement to see, others not so much. The big, white pillars that lined the entrance of the church resembled a usual Southern Baptist church in a small town in the U.S. Brantley looked over at her and winked.

"You ready, sweets?"

She forced herself to smile. "Better now than never." Too bad he truly didn't know how serious that statement was.

They walked with her family inside, and the greeters gave them all bulletins. She recognized the men. Fred and Grover—they were both probably in their mid-eighties now, both World War II vets who never missed a Sunday or a Clemson football game. Both their wives were over weddings, events, charities, and bake sales at the church. They were two of the kindest and wisest old men Lyndie had ever met. They talked to her for a while, almost making Lyndie forget why she was so worried in the first place. But they weren't the problem.

She followed her family into the pew, part of her mind getting excited thinking maybe he didn't go here anymore or was out sick.

"You okay?" Brantley whispered in her ear.

She smiled at him. "Yeah, why wouldn't I be?"

"You looked a little frazzled. Just checking." He squeezed her hand, and she felt her body ease up a little bit. Then all too soon, it froze up again.

She felt like the breath had just been sucked right out of her, and her heart was now in the pit of her stomach. There he was. For the first time in five years, she was seeing the man she had vowed to never see again. He was standing by the stage shaking hands with Pastor Bill. He looked as laid-back and professional as ever. Suddenly, he turned and looked right at her; their eyes met, and he smiled and kept doing what he was doing as if she were just a familiar face that didn't phase him at all.

She started to feel clammy, and right when she was about to escape to the bathroom, Preacher Bill came on stage.

"Good morning, everybody. So glad to have y'all in the Lord's house with us today. Let's stand up and go to him in prayer." Lyndie took a deep breath in, trying to calm down. It was almost a relief for everybody to have their heads bowed and nobody able to see her. She didn't even really hear the prayer. She didn't even hear anything at this point. Once the pastor said amen, she tried to focus on the songs the choir and congregation were singing. Hymns of her childhood—she was hanging onto every word at this point to get her mind off of him. She started to loosen up right when it was time for preaching to begin. Luckily, she hadn't seen where he was sitting, so she looked straight ahead, making sure to not look around. She absolutely hated that she couldn't pay attention to the message. For the most part, she used to enjoy Preacher Bill's sermons. His style was a little old-school, but it always made her leave feeling encouraged and uplifted. However, she already knew this Sunday would be very different from the Sundays spent in Folly at Brantley's church.

After what seemed like three hours, Pastor Bill did an altar call. Brantley made his way to the front, and she watched as he prayed diligently. She was so proud of who he was. Then out of the corner of her eye, she saw him walk up and kneel almost right next to Brantley. This time, instead of feeling like she was having a panic attack, her blood began to boil. This was supposed to be her time with her family and her new boyfriend. Most importantly, this was supposed to be her time with God. She couldn't even focus enough on the sermon or pray when she needed to the most, and then he goes and kneels beside her boyfriend in prayer.

She couldn't help but feel like God was saying to her, "This is what happened before you let him pull you away from Me. You blamed it all on Me, even if you didn't realize it. Don't let him do it again." She felt like she'd been punched in the gut. God was right—she couldn't let him ruin her time of worship just like he had the past five years. She forced herself to close her eyes and sink into a quick prayer. She praised God for giving her the strength to come; she prayed that God would help her to overcome this and thanked Him again for His goodness.

After that, the pastor said a closing prayer, and families started to make a beeline for the door. Unfortunately, her family was a little bit more social.

She felt her gut clench before she could even process it. He was walking up to her. She tried excusing herself, but it was too late.

"Hey, Mike and Sher, how've y'all been?"

She watched as her dad shook his hand. "We're good as always."

Right when she was about to walk away, he turned his attention towards her.

"Lyndie, long time, no see. Hope all is well."

She couldn't even find the air to say a word. She bolted toward the doors. Never in her wildest dreams had she thought he'd act perfectly fine, like he hadn't been the reason she was so damaged. She felt the hot tears start to spill down her face, as she reached the car. Her nerves got the best of her, and she found herself bent over and threw up behind the car. She felt a hand on the small of her back. She said a silent prayer hoping it was Brantley.

"Lyndie, you okay?"

Thank goodness it was Brantley. She couldn't even tell him yes. She was crying so hard. By then, she could hear her parents walking up. What was she going to tell all of them?

After a minute, she finally regained her composure. They didn't even look confused or ask what was wrong; it seemed as though they just all assumed she had the stomach bug, which she would happily go along with. Thankfully, nobody mentioned going out to eat.

After she drank lots of water, her mom said, "If you're sick, you probably don't need to drive back to Charleston today. Brantley probably wants to keep his Jeep throw-up free."

"Um, I'm feeling fine, actually, and he'll be driving. If I start to feel sick, he can pull over." She looked at Brantley, hoping he would pick up on the fact that she wanted to leave, although he didn't know why.

He chimed in. "Yeah, I don't mind. That Jeep has seen a lot worse than puke," he said with a grin.

They said their goodbyes. Lyndie hated that they were departing on such an awkward note, but she didn't know what else to do. She braced herself for the three-and-a-half-hour drive ahead because she knew Brantley wasn't as naive as her parents to think she just got sick. However, she fell asleep without even knowing it twenty minutes into the drive. Brantley didn't wake her until they were coming into Charleston. Her body felt exhausted. Brantley seemed reserved and quiet but still his usual, kind self. To her surprise, he didn't bring up what happened until he pulled up to her apartment. He turned to her and looked her deep in the eyes like he could see right through her.

"So I'm not gonna push, but I would like to know what happened back there. I know you weren't sick, and I know you looked like a ghost when that man walked up."

Lyndie drew in a deep breath. She wanted to tell him so bad; she wanted him to hold her and let her cry out the tears that had been building up inside her for years, but she couldn't, not yet anyways. She thought she'd never tell anybody what happened, but now, she had finally found someone with whom she wanted to share it, just not yet.

"Brantley I'm just not ready yet. I know it's hard to understand, but I do want to tell you. I just need to have some alone time to myself to process it all before I do. Can you understand that?"

He looked ahead like it hurt him to hear her say that, and Lyndie's heart ached.

"No, I want you to tell me when you're ready. But, Lyndie, I don't want secrets between us, not if we are planning on getting more serious."

"I know." Those were the only words she could muster up. She hugged his neck and kissed him, got her stuff, and jumped out. She had a long night ahead of her trying to figure all this out. She had a feeling it would involve a lot of praying and a lot of tears.

24
Brantley

Despite the three-hour drive he had just made, Brantley took the long way home. He was so confused. It had been the perfect weekend, and when Lyndie told him she wanted to go to church that morning, he was so happy. But then something happened. He had no idea what, other than the fact that she didn't have a breakdown until after that guy had walked up. He had caught onto that, and something kept bringing his mind back to it. He didn't want to push her, though—that's why he had let her sleep. And although he planned on asking her more when he had dropped her off, he could see she wasn't ready to talk to him about it. And no matter how hard it was, he had to respect that. He was falling more and more for her every passing day, and everything had been better than he could've ever imagined.

He kept trying to tell himself to not make that much out of it and found himself praying the rest of the drive home. He asked God to prepare both of their hearts for what was to come and for His plans for them. He asked God to give him patience with Lyndie and for him to try to understand and that she would have the strength to tell him what was really going on. He stood by what he said about their relationship going nowhere if she couldn't be honest with him. The thought alone made his heart wince. After feeling a little bit better, he decided he would wait for her to call him because he didn't want to make her feel pressured.

Surprisingly, he fell asleep easily that night and woke the next morning feeling a little more at peace, especially after doing his Bible study. Ironically, it was about Jacob serving for seven years to gain Rachel's hand in marriage. He saw it as a gentle reminder to have patience, especially for those for whom he cared. But as the day crept on, he found this a lot easier said than done. He went to his classes and then to work for a couple of hours; and at seven o'clock, she still hadn't called. He decided to go get pizza with Matt to get his mind off things.

When they sat down, Matt asked him, "So how'd the weekend go?"

"It went all right."

"What happened to make it just all right?"

Brantley shrugged. "Her family was great, and we had a great time until Sunday. I don't know, man. Don't say anything to anyone, but I think she's going through some things that have to do with her past, and she has yet to fill me in on what that is." He paused, and Matt shook his head, as if motioning Brantley to go on. "And I'm trying to be patient and give her the space I feel like she needs, but she just acted real weird when I dropped her off. And she hasn't called me all day."

"And why don't you call her? You're the dude—don't you think that's what she's waiting on?"

"Yeah, I guess I could. I just don't want to suffocate her."

"Do you really think it's something serious going on with her that she just needs to think through?"

"I guess it's a little bit of both."

"You should call her."

Brantley said he would think about it.

Unfortunately, the talk did little to get her off his mind. He still wasn't feeling ready to call her, so he made his way to the beach. He stood in front of the ocean and watched as the waves rolled onto the shore. Other than a light breeze, it was a perfect night. He sat down and stared up at the stars wondering how far they went. Once again, he found himself praying. Some of the best conversations he had with God were right there in front of the ocean at night.

"God, I wanna pray for Lyndie. I don't know what she's going through, but You do. And I pray whatever it is it brings her closer to You and that I can be there for her no matter what it is and whatever happens between me and her. I pray that You've set this all up and You have her on the road You want her on to fall deeply in love with You.

"God, I pray she begins to know You in an intimate way and grows in You. You've helped me through so much, and I couldn't have gotten through all that I have without You. Be there with her the same way, please, God."

He kept talking in a gentle whisper for what ended up being an hour. At some point, he ended his prayer and started talking as if he were talking to his parents. He did this occasionally, as a way to remind himself that they weren't dead; they were, rather, in a different world, a much better world than he was. It kept them real to him. He told them about Lyndie and could feel his eyes start to well up with tears. He told them he wished so badly they could still be here with him and that Grandma and Papa were doing great. When he had nothing more to say, he stared up into the heavens and could feel with all of his heart that somewhere up there, they could hear him, and they were there for him even still.

25

Lyndie

Two days had gone by since Lyndie and Brantley had arrived home from the weekend with her family. She stayed busy and gave herself excuses to not call Brantley. What she didn't expect was that he wouldn't call her himself. By Wednesday, she couldn't take it any longer. She found herself oddly nervous as she waited for him to pick up.

He picked up on the second ring, thankfully. "Hey, there."

"Hey, I'm sorry we haven't talked in a couple of days. I've been so busy, you know, with school and all." She could hear the unsureness even in her own voice.

"Yeah, I know, Lyndie. So, um, how ya been otherwise?"

"I've been okay—no more panic attacks, so that's good."

"Well, do you think you'd wanna get together sometime this week and talk?"

She started to find a reason in her mind why she couldn't but realized it was inevitable.

"How about this Saturday? I could come to Folly, and we could get lunch on the beach or something?"

"Yeah, that sounds good." There was an awkward silence, and then Lyndie told him she'd better go and get started on homework.

She ended the phone call feeling more exhausted than she had before. How was she ever going to explain this to him when she couldn't even deal with it herself?

26
Brantley

The days crept by until Saturday. Brantley barely heard from Lyndie through the rest of the week. He hated feeling like this and was more than ready to have it behind them. He waited outside of his driveway for her to pull in, and when she got out, it was all he could do to not run after her, pick her up, and hold her tight. He remained calm and gave her a sweet hug and kissed her. He missed her familiar smell of coconut and amber.

"You wanna walk to the beach?"

"That sounds good."

He reached for her hand as they walked towards the sand. They took a seat, and both looked out on the horizon. He heard her take a deep breath.

"Okay, so first, you need to know I have never told anyone this. It's unfair for me to keep this from you any longer." She drew another breath before continuing. "I grew up going to my family's church. It was my safe place, and I always couldn't wait until I could go on Wednesday nights. I had so many friends there, and I was close to God—or I thought I was, anyway. This guy named Luke is a big part of the church and always has been."

Brantley didn't even have to ask; he knew the man she was talking about was the one she ran from at church. His stomach began to form into knots. He did not like where this story was headed.

She went on. "At that time, he was probably twenty-eight. He was engaged, and everyone at church loved him and his fiancée. I had never really spoken to him, mostly because of our age difference. Well, he eventually started helping with the youth group, and I always sensed a certain favoritism towards me that he didn't have for anyone else. I was proud of it, thinking it was because he saw me as a leader and a good person. Nothing romantic. He was almost thirty years old, and he was engaged, too. He kept asking me to hang around after or come earlier to help set up stuff for the youth group. I was happy to do it and thought it was because I was responsible or something."

She paused, and only then did Brantley look at her and see the tears starting to fill her eyes as she looked out onto the ocean.

"Brantley, I don't even know how to say this. I look back now and realize I should have caught onto the warning signs, like when he would make flirty comments about how I looked or would stand a little too close when he talked to me when we were alone. But I was naïve then. One day, I stayed after church to help set up for the youth retreat the following weekend. I had no clue he had sent the other kids home, telling everyone to meet back up in the morning to help. I felt someone grab me around the waist from behind. I couldn't even scream. Then he started talking in my ear, telling me stuff he wanted to do to me. I tried pulling away; I tried. Before I knew it, all my strength was gone from fighting him, and I was pinned underneath him. He started to touch me in all my intimate places. I cried like I had never before. I screamed, and nobody came.

It was just me and him, and I was helpless. Then I heard a door slam shut. He jumped up and fixed himself and jerked me up by the arm and into his office and shut the door. To this day, I still don't know who came in the church, but he came back and told me not to ever tell anyone about this. He said what would everyone do if they found out I had thrown myself onto him? A naïve, desperate, sixteen-year-old.

"At that age, I was just stupid enough to believe him when he said that people would trust his story over mine. I ran out and swore I would never step foot back in that church or any church again. How could God even be real if He couldn't protect me from a man I looked up to? A man that we all thought was godly? I realized then it was all fake. Church, Christians—they were just as shameful as any other person. I had been molested in a place that was supposed to be holy and protected by God. I didn't want anything to do with it after that. From that day on, I became a new person. I stopped hanging around my church friends. I became cynical and couldn't wait for the day I graduated and could move away.

"Just when I thought I had moved on and was in a good place, I met you, and everything changed. You're different from him or other people in that church. You don't dress a certain way or do stuff just to be seen by others. You care more about loving me and others and God before everything else. You made me think differently about God and even church. That's why I went back. When I saw him again, I was reminded as I watched how everyone loved and respected him because of his perfect and righteous exterior. And I was a broken and scared, young girl that he took advantage of. He took my innocence, and nobody knows."

For the first time, she looked him in the eyes. He wrapped his arms around her and let her cry for what may have been hours. He knew there were no words he could say at this moment, since God was already saying them to her heart. She had opened up about this to him, and that was one step. He tried to ignore the deep anger that stirred in him, anger like he had never felt before as he felt her body shudder with every tear underneath his arms. When she finally sat up and cried all she could, he wiped her eyes.

"Lyndie, I love you. I love you because of your innocence; that man could never have stolen that from you because God knows that was not what you wanted. He knows you're still his innocent, happy, and carefree girl. That is an evil guy, but you are so much better than that, and you're going to be okay. We will get through this together because God knows, God redeems, and God cares."

She looked so defeated. He knew the effects of the battle still weighed heavily on her, but she was going to be okay. Brantley drove her home that night and slept on her couch after he'd tucked her into bed. He lay there for hours thinking about what to do next. She was right; he shouldn't have gotten away with that.

27

Lyndie

There was no doubt Lyndie felt a load lifted from her shoulders when she told Brantley everything. She had often imagined what it would be like when she told someone about it, but she never thought she would actually get to that point. She slept peacefully that night for the first time in weeks.

28

Brantley

He had never known anger like this. Every fiber in him wanted to hurt this guy. That evening, he caught himself and realized that through all of this, he hadn't gone to God. He took a deep breath and went out on their deck. There was something else he had to come to grips with—the guy was a leader in a church. How could someone be so sick? He was so confused and found himself questioning every person he had looked up to in his church. He couldn't imagine something like that coming out about one of them. No wonder Lyndie had turned away from church, God, and all things religious. She didn't trust them. He had always heard of people in religious roles who were rapists or who had done things in secret they shouldn't do, but it had never hit this close to home. And yet, the girl he was in love with was a victim of it. He replayed all she had said over and over in his head, but not once could he think about it without shuddering. It should still be considered rape. He was disgusted. He tried to figure out what to do from there. He knew her parents needed to know, but Lyndie would have to be the one to tell them that.

29

Lyndie

The next day, Brantley came over and told her what was on his mind. Everything he said caught her off guard. She was planning on telling him and moving on, the secret staying between them. Not once had she even considered telling her parents Even after she explained all this to Brantley, he insisted that she at least think about it. Then when he proceeded to tell her how he wanted her parents to know so they could talk to their pastor about everything, he explained that the man needed to be taken out of the position he was in so nothing like that would happen to someone else, if it hadn't already.

"I've done a lot of praying and thinking about this last night, Lyndie; I just don't think there's another way. I know you don't want people to find out, but it's too serious of a matter to be swept under the rug."

"I know, Brantley, but the thing is I've read up on this, and so many times, the people you tell don't believe you. He's married with a family; it has the possibility of coming back to me, making it look like I hit on him and was just telling lies. I know how these things go. I'm already hurt enough, and I really just want to move on."

Brantley sighed. She could tell he was getting frustrated, but this was her secret that she had kept for years now—she couldn't come to terms overnight with telling the whole world now after so long. She laid her hand on his. "Look, Brant, this is hard for me. I trust you—that's why I told you—but I don't know how to do that with other people. Please just be patient with me."

He gave her a smile. "Okay, babe. Please pray about it, though. I think that is the only way you can truly move on."

"No, it's not. I'm not saying it's not important, but God is the only way I can move on. Meeting you—you helping me come to grips with all this—is what has made me realize that. That's the only way I will ever be able to forgive that man for what he did. God is the only way."

Brantley kissed the brim of her nose and then her lips. His eyes met hers.

"And that's exactly why I love you."

They spent the rest of the evening walking on the cobblestone streets and overlooking Fort Sumter. As the sun set, Brantley held her on their bench. She thought to herself how perfectly God had planted her exactly where she was and how far she had come in two months' time.

30

Lyndie

Lyndie woke up in the middle of the night from a terrible dream. She was walking through the streets of Charleston when girls of all different ages began to follow her. She started to walk faster, but they never lost sight of her. Then she came to a church and started to walk towards it. She turned to see if the girls were still following her, but they had stopped. She looked on at the fear in their eyes as they stared up at the church. They looked at her with pleading eyes, but they never said a word. She wanted to run inside the church so badly because of how uncomfortable they made her, but she felt guilty for leaving them.

Just as she was trying to decide what to do, she saw Luke, the man who had molested her, standing in the doorway of the church, and she heard the cries of all the young girls. To her amazement, she wasn't afraid and felt compassion for all the girls. As the door of the church slammed shut, she woke up.

Lyndie lay in bed and knew that she had her answer. She would have to do something—if not for herself, for all the girls out there who had lost their faith because of situations like the one in which she had found herself.

31

Brantley

Brantley held Lyndie's hand the whole drive back to the Upstate. He could tell she was nervous from the time he picked her up that morning. They chatted, and Brantley kept finding himself praying the entire way there. As they were pulling into her parent's house, her mom and dad came out on the porch waving and looking so delighted that they had surprised them. They had no idea what was coming. Lyndie had only told them they wanted to come visit and had decided they would tell them the rest later.

Brantley parked the car and looked at Lyndie.

"You can do this; I'm right here with you."

She smiled. "I know, thank you."

They met her parents with hugs and smiles like all was well. Once they had settled in and her younger brother left to hang out with friends, Lyndie and Brantley asked her parents if they could talk to them. Brantley could tell that Lyndie's mom was worried and surprised. He didn't know if he should start or if Lyndie should. Right before he was about to begin, Lyndie spoke up.

"Mom, Dad, I really don't know how to say this, so I'm just gonna say it. Something . . . " she paused and looked at Brantley with uncertainty. Then she went on. "Something happened to me when I was sixteen years old that I never told y'all about, and I think I need to now." She went on to relay the same story she had told him that day on the beach. She seemed a lot less comfortable, though, and Brantley could tell she was struggling to get through it. When she finally finished telling the story, he could tell she was about to lose it, along with her mom, so he stepped in.

"I know this is hard to hear. She's been through so much and has been so brave."

Lyndie's mom went over to sit beside her and held her daughter. Her mom looked like she had been punched in the gut. Lyndie's dad had a different reaction. He stormed out of the house, and Brantley went after him. He found him on the porch pacing back and forth with tears streaming down his face.

"If only I could get my hands on that sick man. That's my little girl! And she's had to live with this." He mumbled some other things that took Brantley aback.

"I knew this was going to come as a shock. It came as a shock to me, too."

He looked up at Brantley. "I am her dad. I am supposed to protect her, and I couldn't even do that. I've never liked that guy, and little did I know he had ruined my little girl's life. How could this happen? How could I be so oblivious?" He kicked the side of the porch.

Brantley wasn't sure what to say. "Sir, you had no way of knowing. This isn't your fault."

Mike sighed deeply and looked up at the sky. "And all this time, I thought she just didn't care about going to church or having a relationship with God. Now, I understand she didn't trust Him. She blamed Him."

"But she's come back, and she realizes now that God never left her. I don't think she blames Him anymore."

"Will you ask her to come out here? I need to talk to her alone," her dad said in almost a whisper. Brantley called for Lyndie. He watched as he went back inside to sit with her mom. Lyndie fell into her daddy's arms like a child. They had just shattered her parents' world with this truth, and he prayed that God would heal these wounds.

32

Lyndie

Lyndie slept in the next morning. She had cried so much with her parents the night before that her head was throbbing. She listened to a slight murmur of voices coming from the kitchen. She got ready and went out of her room to find Brantley sitting at the table with both of her parents. They looked like they were in a serious conversation. *Wonder what that could be about,* she thought.

"Hey, honey, come sit with us. There's blueberry pancakes and coffee on the counter," her dad said. Lyndie joined them at the table.

Her dad started. "So I am gonna get right to it. I wanna go see this guy. I want to look him straight in the eyes and tell him what I know. Then I wanna notify the law and, of course, Pastor Bill."

Lyndie took a big gulp of coffee. She knew this was coming, but she didn't know if she was prepared for it.

"I don't know if that's the best way to go about it, Dad. I don't want you to end up doing something to him, and he probably is just gonna deny it anyway. That's a big reason why I haven't told anyone."

Her mom looked frustrated. "Mike, she's right. You could barely keep yourself from going over there all night last night because you wanted to hurt him. I mean, really; how do you think you're gonna be when he's right there in front of you? I just don't know if it's a smart idea at all."

Brantley interjected with caution. "Well, this is just an idea, but what if I talked to him? I don't know him, and he doesn't know me. Y'all can deal with the cops and your pastor, but I could try and handle this guy—at least for the first time."

Lyndie listened to her parents go out and back with Brantley about ideas until they finally agreed Brantley's idea was best. It pained her to listen. Her family was already stressing out because of her. She knew she shouldn't, but she couldn't help but feel guilty.

"I'm gonna go shower and get ready." She stood in the shower for a good thirty minutes, crying and praying through all the fresh wounds that were just now surfacing after so many years of trying to push them down. It bugged her that not once had anyone asked her opinion on what should be done—this was all about her, after all. It was she who had suffered for so many years remembering what happened. It was she who had her innocence stolen in that church that had once been a safe zone for her. These things couldn't be wiped clean by just talking to him and contacting the police department. She realized then that she was finally grieving what happened. She was finally letting herself feel hurt and scared.

She remembered all the Bible verses she had been reading over and over again about forgiveness and how it was having a hard time sinking in. Then she realized she had to feel the effects of what had happened in order to forgive. She had found God again, and He would help her do it. She just wanted her parents to talk about that with her, not just the hard stuff of getting back at him. She had to figure out a better way.

33

Brantley

Later that day, Lyndie explained, "Look, if it were up to me, I would pack up and head back to Charleston and act like all this had never happened. But I can't, not after this dream I had the other night. I have to stop this so no other girls have to go through what I did, or worse. So I will let you talk to him if it gives you peace of mind. If he doesn't fess up to it and if the pastor and police do nothing about it, I'm gonna handle it. It's the only way, and it's not about revenge. It's about protecting other people from this."

Brantley listened as the tears welled up in her eyes.

"Okay, I promise I won't get in the way." He spent the rest of the afternoon trying to keep Lyndie entertained while her parents met with the police and then their pastor. He held her hand as they walked around the botanical gardens in Clemson and listened as she talked about their future. Even in the midst of tragic circumstances, she still let off an inner peace that radiated to his soul.

"Do you think my parents will ever look at me the same?"

"Why do you think they would look at you any differently?"

Lyndie looked down at her hands. "I don't know. I guess I'm afraid they'll start seeing me differently, like I've lost my innocence or that I'm a victim or something. I just want them to still see me as independent. I don't want them to be worried about me."

"I'm not gonna lie; they probably will be worried for a long time, just because this is new to them, even if it isn't to you. But they are your parents, and it's their job to worry about you. You're still innocent. Anyone who knows you and knows your heart sees that God made you as pure as they come, and nothing and no one can change that because you're a daughter of the King."

Lyndie kissed him and whispered how much she loved him in his ear. All he could think was how that would never get old.

They could see both her parents sitting at the table when they pulled into the driveway. They looked serious, and Brantley began to worry. They greeted them at the door and tried to make small talk, asking what they did and even commenting on how lovely the weather had been. Brantley knew it hadn't gone well by how they were avoiding the inevitable.

"Okay, Mom, Dad, how did it go?" Lyndie eventually cut in.

Lyndie's parents looked at each other. "It didn't go like we expected it to, baby," Lyndie's dad said.

Her mom went on. "We had our meeting with Pastor Bill first, and he seemed very . . . " She paused and looked at Mike. " . . . concerned. He asked how we knew you were telling the truth."

Mike intervened. "And we assured him that we know our daughter, and she would never make something like this up. And he said that he simply could not make any drastic actions about something like this because there was no evidence as far as he was concerned. He just kept claiming that Luke was a family man, a church leader, and a man of the Lord."

To Brantley's surprise, Lyndie didn't look the least bit shocked. She looked like they were just telling her information she already knew.

"And the police?" she asked.

"They gave us these packets to fill out for a claim of rape and some quote, unquote, good counseling services for girls that experienced some form of sexual assault. However, they said a lot goes into this, and they can't simply arrest or accuse someone of assaulting a girl when it happened four years ago, and there's no proof, and, um . . . " Her dad cleared his throat.

Her mom took the lead. "And since it wasn't actual intercourse to make it rape." Her parents took the next forty minutes to assure her that they believed her and that something would be done. All the while, Brantley knew Lyndie had made her decision as to what she was going to do about it.

34

Brantley

The following day, Lyndie sat with Brantley as they discussed the plans for the day ahead. Brantley was trying to talk her into letting him go talk to Luke today.

"I just don't see what good it is going to do," Lyndie said.

"I want to see what this guy says. I want to know he feels remorse for this or has changed. I don't know, Lyndie. I just don't know what else to do, and I have to do something."

Lyndie groaned aloud. "Okay, but really, I would rather not know how it goes because I know it won't go well."

Brantley gave her a kiss on the forehead and assured her everything was going to be all right.

As Brantley drove to the church, he realized he had no idea what he would say if Luke was even there. That was another problem; what if he wasn't? Brantley found himself getting nervous but pushed the feelings away. He had to at least show Lyndie he would always stand up for her. He found himself praying as he drove down the old back roads.

"God, I don't know what I am about to get myself into or what I am even gonna say. Please give me the words. Please help me to not be overcome with anger or to do anything stupid. I need you to be a part of this, not for me but for Lyndie."

He continued to pray until he pulled into the old brick church he had come to with Lyndie and her family. He sat in his Jeep for a good five minutes trying to gather his thoughts and finally made his way up to the doors of the church. Luckily, the doors were unlocked, and he walked in. An older man greeted him at the door. He recognized him from the last time he was there as the pastor.

"Well, hello, young man, can I help you with something?"

Brantley couldn't help but notice how thick his southern accent was.

"Yeah, I am Lyn—" he stopped himself, remembering how Lyndie's parents talk with him had gone yesterday. "I'm looking to see if Luke is here."

"Actually, I think he just got here—he should be down in the deacon's office or in the youth room." The pastor stopped himself. "Is he expecting you?"

Despite Brantley's morals, he came up with a quick white lie. "I wanted to surprise him; we are old friends." As soon as he said this, he immediately regretted it. Here he was, lying in a church, to a pastor; this was already starting out on a bad note.

Luckily, the pastor seemed to relax. "All right, son, go on down. Let me know if I can help you with anything else."

"Yes, sir, thank you very much."

He felt bad about his little white lie, especially in church, but God had to understand, right? Brantley heard booming laughter coming from an office downstairs. He saw through the crack of the door the man who came and talked to Lyndie's family when he was last at church. His stomach began to flop with disgust. He cleared his throat and took a step in the doorway. Luke was on the phone when he looked up and saw Brantley; he didn't seem to recognize him and held up a finger to give him a minute.

"Yes, sir, wife's doing well; so are the kids. If you need anything else for your ministry, please let me know—you know I am always happy to help."

After what seemed like ages, he hung up. "All right. Sorry about that, sir; what can I help you with?"

Brantley discreetly turned on the recorder on his phone. "May I have a seat please?"

"Sure. I don't believe I know you; you must be new to the church."

"No, actually, I don't go here." Brantley took a deep breath. He needed to just get right to it. "I am Lyndie Pruett's boyfriend."

Without even skipping a beat, Luke smiled. "Ah, how is she? We haven't seen much of her since she moved down to Charleston."

"I think you know why you haven't seen much of her in the past four years, and I think you know that's why I am here."

A confused look spread across his face. "I am sorry. I don't believe I know what you are talking about."

With a stern look on his face, Brantley persisted to speak to him with as much patience as he could muster "Lyndie has opened up to me and her parents about what you did to her. I am here to tell you that if you don't admit to this and resign from your position, there's gonna be consequences."

Luke folded his hands together and looked Brantley square in the eyes. "I don't believe that's why you are here. I think you're here because you wanted to know the truth because you are not sure if you believe her." Before Brantley could interject, Luke went on. "It seems like you have been horribly misinformed by an attention-starved young lady. Yes, I knew Lyndie but not the Lyndie you seem to know. I was fairly new as a youth minister then, and I remember how she would flirt with all the boys and was constantly changing boyfriends week by week. Then she started to become a little too friendly for my comfort. I had a fiancée, so at first, I tried to tell myself I was looking too much into it. She was a young girl, and I was engaged—surely she wasn't coming onto me."

Brantley felt the blood vessels in his head tighten and his fists clench.

"Then one Sunday after church, I was trying to get all my stuff ready to leave church, and she came into the room and closed the door behind her and persisted to come onto me and kiss me. Of course, I pushed her off and told her that she was a child and that I had a fiancée. I told her to go home. She then told me she would tell everyone I raped her if I didn't love her back. I then ran out myself, and I have tried to forget about it ever since. You see, I wanted to believe she had changed and that it was just her young immaturity coming out; I try my best to see the best in people."

Brantley could not believe what he had just heard. He automatically jumped up.

"You're such a liar. I know Lyndie, and none of that is true. You know you molested her! You're sick. You ruined her life, and you do not deserve to be in this position; and I am gonna see to it that you face even bigger consequences than losing your job." Brantley realized he was yelling by this point and could hear footsteps coming down the hall. The pastor stepped in.

"What's all this about?"

Brantley knew he had to leave. He turned one last time and watched a fake smile come across Luke's face.

"Sometimes, the truth is hard to hear."

Brantley just about lost it and jerked his arm out from the pastor's hand.

"Now, you can't come here accusing one of my men of things they didn't do."

Brantley faced him. "Believe what you want, but remember that the devil was an angel before he fell. Maybe you need to take a second look at who you choose to lead your church instead of condemning innocent girls."

At that, Brantley walked out and slammed the door shut. Without a doubt, this was the angriest he had ever been in his life. He drove around for the next hour not knowing where he was, praying, thinking. That guy was messing with his head—how had he let himself lose control like that? He was normally the calm, cool guy. How was he going to tell Lyndie about what had happened? He was only making the mess bigger.

35

Lyndie

Brantley didn't even have to tell her his talk with Luke had gone badly. She knew by the way he was acting when he got back to the house. He was avoiding everything but telling her what was said. When finally she could not take it any longer, she flat out asked him, "So, Brantley, you gonna tell me how it went? You've been acting nervous ever since you got back."

"I really don't want to lie to you or hurt your feelings, so I'm just gonna say it; he told me that you came onto him, and he told you no. He said that you had become wild and were dating a new guy every week."

Although Lyndie expected it, she was still surprised at the hurt she felt knowing that was said. "Okay, you don't believe him, do you?"

Brantley held her hand. "Of course not. I could tell the guy was a creep before I even sat down."

"What did Pastor Bill say to you?"

"What makes you think he said anything to me?"

"You're ignoring the question."

"All he really said was that I had no business coming around accusing his workers. Which I guess you were right—I didn't think it through, and I'm sorry for that."

Lyndie felt numb. Even as much as she talked to Brantley about her plan, she really didn't want it to come to that. She had hoped, even prayed, that Brantley's talk with him would have worked. Why did she feel like she needed to finish something? Why couldn't she move on and feel peace? It was like a nagging feeling that God still wasn't done with this yet, and she was afraid it would take her being brave to do it. "You know this means I am gonna have to talk to him myself."

"Lyndie, not by yourself."

"Brantley it's not up to you, and besides, he won't let his guard down if someone else is around."

"But what makes you think he will be with you? He knows that you are out to get him. Why would he trust you?"

"I honestly am not sure that he will, but I feel like I need to try this. It's about the only thing we have left."

They heard her parents come out on the porch, and they both quickly changed the subject. But Lyndie couldn't help but think, *What am I getting myself into?*

36

Brantley

He hated that they had to keep this a secret from Lyndie's parents. They were trying their best to help, but he could tell all they were really doing was frustrating her even more. He knew he would have to go back to Charleston soon; his work had given him two days off during the week, and they had planned to stay through the weekend, then go back. Today was Sunday and was going to be their last day there.

"When are you planning on doing it?" Brantley asked Lyndie.

"I don't know. I was thinking today, but I feel like I need more time. I would have no idea what to say."

Brantley tried to have patience. "I understand, but you can't get behind in your schoolwork. You are about to graduate, and so am I. We need to go back to Charleston."

Lyndie paused without saying anything for a second. "I know you're right. I will think of something. Let's just eat with my parents when they get out of church, and then we can head back."

Brantley looked at her almost in disbelief that she had given in so easy. "Are you sure?"

Lyndie nodded. "It's okay. We need to get back. I know that. I guess I just got a little caught up in this. I forgot about the real world."

"Okay, well, do you wanna go to church somewhere else today?"

"Actually, I think I would like to go with my parents."

To their surprise, when they went into the kitchen, her parents were still in their pajamas—very unusual for a Sunday morning.

"Mom, Dad, are y'all not going to church?" Lyndie asked.

They both looked at one another. "Hun, you didn't really think we could go back there with everything that we have found out?"

"Guys, please don't stop going to church there. Y'all love that place. Please."

"There is no way I could go there anymore, Lyndie," her dad said sternly.

"What if I told y'all I wanted to go, that I needed to go, and I think it will be good for me to face him?"

They looked taken aback. "Why? How could that possibly be good for you?" Lyndie's mom asked.

"That way, I can move on. That way, y'all don't stop going to the church you love over one man."

"But it's more than just that. We told Pastor Bill and even some of the other deacons, and they basically told us they didn't believe you or us."

"Mom, Dad, think about it—out of the blue, he has an accusation on one of his deacons he has always thought to be a saint or something. That's a hard thing to believe. Who would want to believe one of their employees, especially one who works for a church, would do that?"

"I don't know. He could've at least sounded a little more concerned or looked more into it."

"Please go—at least today—for me," Lyndie asked.

They hesitated for a moment. "If it means that much to you, although I think it's crazy, we will," her dad said.

37

Lyndie

She knew they all were concerned about her wanting to go to church this morning, so she tried to not let them see how nervous she actually was. She spent all morning praying as she got ready. *God, please help me do this.* She felt she had said this a million times. Luckily, they got to church two minutes late, so everyone was already sitting down when they walked in, and they took a place on the back pews.

As soon as Lyndie sat down, she noticed him sitting second row with his arm wrapped around his wife. She watched how he nodded to everything the pastor said, and she tried to tell herself there had to be good in him. She felt bad because she couldn't pay attention to the service. As much as she tried, her anxiety took her elsewhere. When the service began to draw to an end, she really began to get nervous. Then the final amen was said, and everybody got up and started chatting or rushed out to get lunch.

"I am going to go say hey to Emily; I think she told me she was going to be in the nursery," said Lyndie.

She caught a weird glance from Brantley and was afraid he knew what she was doing but hoped he wouldn't show it if he did.

"Okay, honey. Well, we will probably head on out to the car, so you can just meet us out there," her dad said with obvious hesitation.

"Okay. I'll see y'all out there." As she turned, she saw Luke heading downstairs, alone. She followed behind, hoping no one would stop her or pay her any attention.

The dim and cold hallway reminded her of her childhood, how she used to see church as a fun place to see her friends at VBS or youth group lock-ins. The musky scent brought back many memories, both good and bad. She stopped at the end of the hall, remembering where his office was, and turned on the recorder on her phone. She forced herself forward, as if her mind and body were two totally separate things, because if her mind was controlling her body right now, she would still be standing frozen at the end of the staircase.

She cleared her throat and then knocked. He looked a little shocked when he saw her standing at the door. Then a quick smile spread across his face. Before she could even get a word out, he said in a loud, booming voice, "Lyndie! It's been so long. How have you been?" She couldn't even believe this. How could he act so cool?

"We need to talk." It was the only thing she could think to say.

Luke looked at his watch. "Well, right now isn't really a good time—my family is waiting on me to go eat."

With all the courage inside her, she mustered up the words. "Well, you need to make time. I think you know what I'm here about. What you did to me was wrong. And you've denied it to my family and my boyfriend; but you and I both know what really happened, and you can't deny it with me. You ruined my life, and more importantly, you ruined my relationship with God." Without missing a beat, she kept going. "And you call yourself a deacon or a man of God. You ruined me! I am just now facing this, and I am gonna ask you before this gets any worse to step down because you are in no place to be working in a church or with kids; you need help." "Lyndie, I think it's time to tell yourself and your family the truth. I don't know if you want to keep it a secret from your new boyfriend that you came onto a married man, but the way you've twisted this story has me worried about your own mental health. Now I have moved on; I didn't want to get you in trouble. I was hoping you would have moved on, too. I would hate for the church to find out what really happened."

She was speechless. There was no point in even trying. Just about that time, she heard a woman calling out Luke's name coming down the hallway.

"Luke, there you are; we're waiting on you," said the woman as she came into his office. Then she saw Lyndie and looked at her strangely. "Oh, hey, Lyndie; it's been a while. How are you?"

Luke interjected, "She just came in to say hello. I am ready now, honey. After you, Lyndie."

Lyndie practically ran up the stairs. She felt so helpless; there was nothing she could do. The horrible thoughts about him came rushing back, and she thought over and over about how much she never wanted to see that evil man again.

38

Brantley

That evening, Brantley listened intently as Lyndie told him what had happened. He held her tight and told her he loved her and that God would make this right, even though deep down, he was beginning to question that himself. Lyndie caught him off guard when she asked, "You do believe me, right?"

"Lyndie, why would I not believe you over that creep? Don't ever think that." He kissed her softly on her lips.

"Thank you for everything. I guess I just really thought God wanted me to do something about this, but I don't know; maybe I was wrong."

"Remember it's in His timing, not our own. I know it hurts when we feel like we have no control of a situation, but I have to believe he has a plan."

"But what if it's not in this lifetime? I can't help but think what if God is just gonna punish him for it—you know, on Judgment Day or something."

"I can't say I know exactly what He's doing; but I know He is a just God, and He knows the best way to deal with this guy, even if it is in Heaven. Trust him, honey."

"Will you pray with me or, well, for me? For direction and peace even if there's no justice that comes out of this?"

"I would love that."

That evening, they prayed together for over thirty minutes. Brantley couldn't help thinking over the idea of asking Lyndie to marry him as he lay in bed that night. He knew they hadn't been together for very long, but he knew that he loved her and that God had put her in his life for a reason.

39

Lyndie

Lyndie woke up that next morning having decided she was ready to go back to Charleston and get on with her life. She felt a peace that had not been there the night before. She felt that God would do what needed to be done. She explained the news to her family. Surprisingly, they all agreed and went on eating breakfast together like all was right.

"Are you wanting to leave today?" Brantley asked her.

"How about tomorrow? I was gonna get lunch with an old friend today and was thinking you could take Dad and my brother to go play golf or something?"

"Sounds good to me. I'm proud of you, Lyndie; you're an amazing girl, and I am a lucky guy."

She smiled. It was amazing to her how he still gave her butterflies like when they first met. She busied herself with hanging out and enjoying her family during the day. Sadie was an old high school friend who had always been close. They had met at church, and once she stopped going, they sort of drifted apart until Sadie saw Lyndie at church the other Sunday and texted her and asked if she wanted to get together. She was excited to get to spend some time with Sadie; it had been so long since they last hung out.

The whole way to the restaurant, Lyndie couldn't help but feel a little bit nervous that the conversation would be awkward and they would have nothing to talk about anymore. All those worries washed away when she saw her friend standing outside the restaurant at the mall waiting on her. They both hugged each other and exclaimed how much they missed the other. During dinner, the conversation was light as they talked about Brantley and Sadie's college boyfriend and about their future and the past four years. Lyndie was thoroughly enjoying herself until Sadie's tone changed.

"Lyndie, wanting to catch up wasn't the only reason I asked you to meet me. I um, I actually wanted to talk to you about something— something rather serious, I guess."

"Of course. Is everything okay?"

"Yeah life is good—now, anyway. I really don't know how to say this because I haven't ever told anyone this before. Lyndie, do you remember our old youth pastor, Luke?"

Lyndie's stomach immediately turned. "Yes, I do."

Tears welled up in Sadie's eyes. "Lyndie, he touched me inappropriately multiple times after or before different events we would have. Every time, he would say he would tell everyone that I was trying to get with him if I ever told or if I didn't do what he said." Then the tears that were so familiar to Lyndie started pouring. "I don't know . . . I don't know what else to say." Lyndie looked around as people were beginning to stare, and she knew that would only make it harder on both of them.

"Sadie, is it okay if we go out to my car? I need to tell you something, too."

Through the next hour and a half, Lyndie poured her heart out to Sadie. She described what took place between her and Luke. Sadie looked stunned the whole time. She could tell she had no idea. They cried and hugged one another for a long time. God had sent her a friend, someone who understood, and it came at the perfect time.

"You know, I had almost given up, and then today, God showed me why it's so important that I don't."

Later that day, Lyndie got a call from Sadie. "Hey, Lyndie, I just got to thinking about what you said and all that about why it is important that the church finds out about what he did. And, well, I think I have an idea. You said he knew that you were trying to get him in trouble, but I'm guessing he doesn't know we still talk or know each other's stories."

"No, surely not," Lyndie replied, not sure where she was going. Sadie proceeded to tell her the plan. Lyndie felt like there was a possibility for something to be done again. She heard Brantley outside her door. She hated to keep secrets from him, but she didn't want to tell him. For some reason, she felt she was nervous for what might come from this. So she decided she would keep it between herself and Sadie.

That evening, she and Sadie met up again. Lyndie had told Brantley it was Sadie's birthday dinner and that she needed to spend some time with her before she and Brantley went back to Charleston. Lyndie was nervous but had some amount of peace. She had been praying all morning long and knew that if God wanted this to be revealed, it would be. She felt like they were doing the right thing. Sadie looked as nervous as Lyndie felt.

"Are you sure you're ready?"

"Yes. I'm more than ready," replied Sadie. They drove to the church replaying their plan over and over. When they got there, dusk was starting to set in, and there was a lone blue Ford Fusion in the parking lot, which they knew belonged to Luke. *So far so good*, Lyndie thought to herself.

"So I am going to stay in the car while you are in there," Lyndie told Sadie.

"Okay, here goes nothing."

Lyndie watched as Sadie walked up to the church door and into the building. She said a silent prayer that everything would work out the way it was supposed to and that God would be with Sadie. Now it was up to Lyndie to wait anxiously.

40

Sadie

Sadie tried not to let Lyndie see how nervous she was as she entered the church. Most of the lights were out since everybody had already gone home, except one light downstairs coming from an office. She collected herself and walked to the office and lightly tapped the door.

He looked surprised.

"Hey, Luke, are you busy?"

He smiled at her. "Nothing that I can't put off. What's up? Have a seat."

Instead of taking a seat, Sadie walked closer to him as rehearsed.

"I need to talk to you."

He smiled again, as if to say, *Keep talking.*

"For the past couple of years, I have had you on my mind. I know we have an age difference, but ever since, *you know,* I just felt this connection with you I can't get past. I am gonna be totally upfront with you. Do you think there could ever be a future for the two of us?"

He looked at her skeptically and got up and sat on the edge of his desk with his arms crossed. "Where is all this coming from?"

"I guess I just figured you felt the same way since that happened."

"I see."

"I know your wife doesn't know, and I promise I won't tell. I know it was years ago, and I was so young, but didn't you have feelings for me?"

"No, Sadie I did not. I think you need to leave."

She placed her hand on his. "But, Luke, I need to know if there will ever be a chance."

He looked up at her, and something changed in his eyes. He stroked her cheek. "What if we just kept us a little secret?"

"Okay, but you have to make a deal with me. It can't be like it was the last time. It can't be forced." She took a step closer. "I want it to be mutual this time."

He smiled. "Deal."

"And you won't hurt me again or hold me down?"

"Of course not."

"Okay, then." She smiled. "Would you like to go on a trip this weekend?"

"I might be able to swing it."

"Okay, well I have to go, but here is my new number." She slipped him a piece of paper with a made-up number on it. "I gotta go, but I'll be seeing you."

"Wait." Before she could walk out, he grabbed her arm. "Where are you going?"

"I have to get home to let my dog out." She tried not to look him in the eye.

"You're not going to tell anyone about that other time either, right?"

"Of course not."

"Then do something for me." He jerked her inside the office again.

"You just promised it wouldn't be like that again."

"It won't be. But I just need you to prove something to me."

She felt her heart race. He grabbed a hold of her arm and looked at her suspiciously. She grabbed her keys and pressed the panic alarm. As they heard the car alarm go off, he released his hold of her.

Suddenly, they heard footsteps running down the hall. Lyndie, Pastor Bill, and Brantley all burst through the door.

Pastor Bill took the lead. "What's going on here? I got a call that there was a burglary, and I got here to find Lyndie telling me I needed to get inside quickly." He then looked at Sadie. "Sadie, what are you doing here so late?"

It was then that Sadie pulled the recorder out of her pocket and handed it to him. "I think you need to hear this."

Luke looked like he had seen a ghost. He lunged for the recorder, but Brantley stepped in and pushed him against the wall.

"I think your best move here would be to go home to your family while you still have one."

"They are liars!" he screamed. "They framed me."

"We'll let this be the judge of that," Lyndie said. Luke grabbed his keys and stormed out.

"Pastor Bill, I think you may wanna sit down," Sadie said.

They replayed the recording, and both girls watched as disgust and shock washed over both Pastor Bill and Brantley's faces.

Pastor Bill then looked up at Lyndie. "Lyndie, you tried telling me; I am so very sorry. I had no idea he was capable of something like this. I'm not sure what to do next."

"We aren't sure we were the only ones. We have to contact the police."

"I suppose you're right. I'm sorry. I am still in such shock."

41

Lyndie

They all went to the police department, where Lyndie's parents met them and filed a report using the recorder as proof. After hours of paperwork and recounting the worst thing to ever happen to her, Lyndie fell to pieces in the car with Brantley. He held her tight.

"It's all okay now. It's going to be okay."

"I would've never done this without you. I feel as if I have had a huge weight lifted off my shoulders that's been stationed there for years."

Brantley kissed her forehead. "You'll never have to worry about him again. I am so proud of you for being so brave."

Lyndie was glad she had made that decision sitting in the car to call Brantley and tell him what was going on just in case something were to go wrong. He had insisted on coming up there, and now she understood God knew she would need him there. That night, she slept with a peace she hadn't felt in a very long time. She cried and cried, praising God for making a way when there seemed to be no way. He really does turn everything for good, and she was glad her scars were finally healing.

Epilogue

The sun shone on the water as Brantley and Lyndie sat on their island. It was the day after graduation, and Brantley had decided to take her on a picnic to celebrate.

"So, what's up next?" Brantley asked, wrapping his arms around her.

"Get a job at a school around here. And I think I want to volunteer somewhere helping other girls who have been sexually assaulted. I feel like I am finally in a good place to start telling my story." She looked over at him. "What about you?"

"Hopefully start working at that marine conservation place I told you about. But there is one thing I have to figure out."

"And what might that be?"

"What's up next for us?" He gave her a sly grin.

"I could get used to having you around, I guess." She smiled and looked out into the ocean.

Brantley got up on his knee and pulled out a ring. "In that case, will you marry me?"

Lyndie was completely blown away. Tears filled her eyes. "Are you serious? Oh my goodness, a million times yes."

Brantley picked her up and spun her around. He had never felt so blissful in all his life. They kissed and told one another how much they loved each other. There was no one else Brantley would want to share his life.

Later that evening, as they were walking the island one last time before they had to go, Brantley stopped. He had never noticed the carving on the side of the tree before. He walked closer to see the words "Ray and Leslie" inscribed in the tree. Lyndie came up behind him.

"Is that . . . " Lyndie paused before letting him respond.

Brantley nodded his head. "That's my parents." Brantley thought of that as being his parents' blessing on him and Lyndie. He couldn't help but think how amazing it was the way God's plans played out before their eyes.

For more information about
Megan Ashley Powell
and
Scars that Heal
please visit:

www.meganashley.org

Ambassador International's mission is to magnify the Lord Jesus Christ
and promote His Gospel through the written word.

We believe through the publication of Christian literature, Jesus Christ and
His Word will be exalted, believers will be strengthened in their walk with
Him, and the lost will be directed to Jesus Christ as the only way of salvation.

For more information about
AMBASSADOR INTERNATIONAL
please visit:

www.ambassador-international.com
@AmbassadorIntl
www.facebook.com/AmbassadorIntl

*Thank you for reading, and please consider leaving us a review
on Amazon, Goodreads, or our websites.*

More from Ambassador International

Willow Rysen has been Miss Popular ever since starting high school. But when she is forced to partner with a nerd, Christian Blythe, for a science project that debates the Bible versus science, her world is turned upside down. Will she find that the grace of God can overcome her past failures or will she allow the lure of the world's ideologies to keep her tight in its grasp?

Fred Thorne must shoulder the full care and protection of his sisters after a fire leaves them homeless and friendless. He sets out to follow the last advice given to him by his great-aunt: Take the girls to Menevace, to the refuge home. But the road to Menevace is fraught with bandits, famine, and unknown dangers. Can the Thornes find a place of rest and safety? Will their journey ever end?

Abandoned as infants, Tovi and her twin brother were raised by an eclectic tribe of warm, kind people in a treehouse village in the valley. After her brother's sudden disappearance Tovi questions her life and her faith in an invisible King. Ignoring her best friend Silas' advice, she decides to search for her brother in the kingdom on top of the mountain. Amidst the glamour of the kingdom above the cloud Tovi is torn between her own dark desires and unanswered questions.

www.ingramcontent.com/pod-product-compliance
Lightning Source LLC
Chambersburg PA
CBHW060124260626
47160CB00005B/2009